From One Christmas to the Next

K.G. WATSON

Copyright © 2020 K.G. WATSON

Pandamonium Publishing House

www.pandamoniumpublishing.com/shop

All rights reserved. This book may not be reproduced or stored in any manner, digitally or otherwise without prior written permission of the publisher. All resemblance to characters, living or dead, places, events, and names is purely coincidental and is a product of the author's imagination.

ISBN: 9781989506264

DEDICATION

To Maryella Legatt
whose challenge inspired this book
and to
Letitia Brasovan
who was midwife at the birth of the story

FROM ONE CHRISTMAS TO THE NEXT

For additional titles from Pandamonium Publishing House
please visit our website
www.pandamoniumpublishing.com/shop

"Education gives sobriety to the young, comfort to the old, riches to the poor, and is an ornament to the rich."

-Diogenes

1

He hadn't counted on going in. He'd just been too darned lonely house-sitting the place while its owner studied overseas. He really resented the inane or gratuitously violent TV offerings. So, after his TV dinner, he'd just gone out, walking, till he got tired enough to sleep - just like every other night for the past six months. But who counted?

He had seen the bustle from a block away. Cars had been trying to get into the plugged parking lot. Lines of bundled up families chatted excitedly and called to each other as they converged. Bright light bathed the spire and filled the windows. He found himself trapped between clumps of people ahead and behind and fenced in by the solid row of parked cars to his left. The human tide simply herded him off the sidewalk with them and up the broader approach to the double doors.

Rather than step out of the line into the knee-deep snowbanks he decided he'd just go with the flow. It wasn't that he didn't know the drill. It was Christmas Eve. How many similar services had he conducted through his lifetime? It's just he couldn't do it anymore.

And he had nobody to not do it with either since Margaret had died back in the Spring.

The memory brought the image the Remembrance Cards the Funeral Home had produced. She had always demanded she be referred to as 'Margaret' never 'Maggie'. A moment when he had called her that as he sang an old song about being young had set off an unexpected explosion.

"I was named Margaret and that is the name on my Birth Certificate, and my Driver's License and my bloody Passport," she had shouted. "Get used to it!" She'd never sworn before or after.

"OK," he said to himself halfway up the walk. *"What else is there to do tonight, anyway?"*

Most of the group ahead turned towards a side entrance - probably the Christian Education Wing or something similar - big gym, meeting rooms, kitchen, likely the church office. They left a pair of animated adults right in front of him. One pulled open the main door to let his partner enter and the two couples behind him all but pushed him inside. He took two more steps forward and the group closed ranks behind him - a solid wall of backs in wool worsted.

He reflexively pulled off his toque as he stepped through the inner vestibule doors into the sanctuary. Belatedly, he noticed he had passed the cloakrooms to the right and left just behind him. He had opened his coat. He'd be OK. At that moment he just wanted to get out of the road of the people now fanned out behind him. Three large steps got him into a pew with an aisle seat. A mother tugged a child closer to her, leaving the seat open. When she gave his tousled hair, last cut six months ago, and his three-day stubble a second look, she moved the child to her other side giving as much space as possible between them and the vagrant she obviously thought he was.

Against the flow of new worshippers, an usher pushed towards him and handed him the Order of Service. He held it up to the mother next to him but she showed her own in response. No need to touch anything from him.

He leaned back after a glance at the decorative angels on the cover. It brought instant bile to his throat. When his wife died in the Spring his parishioners had said, so often that she had gone to be with the angels.

"What a stupid thing to say," he had finally burst out. "She was dust and returned to it. She lives only in our memories. There is no heavenly garden party going on." He'd never said such things before.

"It's the trauma of losing his spouse," sympathetic listeners had said. "He will see God's wisdom soon." Didn't happen.

He peeked behind the Christmas cover. The details were all he would have put in. Cast members for The Story were listed - Janine Walters, at two months old, got credit for being Baby Jesus. That made him chuckle. By the time he had finished his scan of the program, a child, with an adult at his elbow, had finished lighting the thick candles in the holders attached to the pews all the way from the front and was doing the last on the pew ahead of him. The child's high stretch to touch the wick with the lighter was followed intently by his minder. When both candles lifted flames upward, they extinguished the lighter and made their way back to the front. Within moments, the harsh electric glare gave way to a muted yellow and shadowy gloom. Showtime.

Almost immediately, the candles overhead guttered frantically as the lead members of the choir entered the vestibule on a gust of wind. He could see the back end of the line-up through the side windows of the chancel as they scurried up the outside walkway, ready to process. From the speaker system a loud voice read from Isaiah 9:6 "For unto us a child is born, unto us …". Searing lances of light shot from projectors onto large screens at the front. The organ swelled and the choir lurched into step as they sang "O Come Molly Faithful."

The congregation sang the right words clearly displayed on the screens. He just couldn't help thinking of the corruption. Closely behind the choir, as they gathered in the chancel, was an unscripted character, frantically searching for seats. He beckoned late-comers, singly or pairs from where they were queued. Into the space ahead of him slid a beautifully dressed woman - late thirties early forties, he guessed. The beige, felted bycocket hat was what Robin Hood wore but this had a rakish slash of pheasant feather. From beneath the hat, a smooth blond coiffure peaked out, every hair in place. It was her fur coat that stopped traffic. It was likely mink, wide-lapelled, a dazzling gold broach. She slid into place during the 'Amen' and sat gracefully.

Mary and Joseph had appeared at this elbow in another wind gust. The two-child donkey brought up the rear. While they walked slowly up the center aisle, a cluster of shepherds in bathrobes appeared on stage left.

"And suddenly there was with the angel, a multitude of the heavenly host proclaiming ...," declared the narrator.

"Glory to God ...," raggedly declared the choir with full organ.

As the young shepherds skipped up one side aisle and back on the other, the choir finished. The peasants were in place on cue to adore Baby Jesus who had suddenly appeared in the crèche.

The service continued for him on autopilot. *"These people really believed this happened,"* he thought. *"Don't they know it is just a story Matthew, or whoever, made up. It's a terrific story sure and it has stood the test of time. But it was not a news report. If you wanted to be important in that day, you had to be a firstborn, had to be born miraculously, had to have supernatural cheerleaders. The story they were acting out didn't happen. It was written a century after the event and had a whole different purpose - politics."*

He was the evidence that people did, in fact, think they were repeating history. When he had declared the benefits of centuries of biblical study to his flock, he had found his 'Call' was withdrawn. That is why he had left his congregation - fired - by truths no one wanted to hear and by hard leaders who were heard. And the Chair of the Board's wife wore a coat exactly like the one sitting in front of him.

With each entry of the magi, the candles in front of him flared and thrashed about hysterically. In fact, the ones above the mink coat had created large wells of liquid around the wicks. They would surely pour down on the poor woman if the thin walls holding them were breached. He touched her shoulder to warn her as they were standing for the last hymn.

The stir of people rising, flicked the flame just enough to do what he feared. He caught the movement peripherally as he was reaching forward. He jammed his program upward as he pushed the lady sideways into her neighbours. Hot wax burned his thumb but the paper caught and diverted the first molten blob. The lady turned and shrieked at the rough man who had tried to take her coat, just as the congregation broke into song. She clutched her coat to her with one hand and stared at him in terror, her other arm lifted in defense. A seat mate pulled her away. "As with gladness men of old …" the congregation sang. Few noticed the discord but strong hands quickly grabbed him from behind and pulled him towards the vestibule.

"I was trying to catch the wax," he had explained to the usher over the music. He showed his reddened, wax-covered skin.

"Put out those candles. They'll hurt someone."

The man looked back uncertainly. The second candle's pool of wax dribbled suddenly. Both long exposed wicks blazing threateningly. Another usher had seen the same thing and was carrying a chair into place. He needed hands to steady him as he reached to pinch out the flame.

"Stay away from her," the attendant ordered and turned to help his friend.

"Amen."

The congregation had been invited to share refreshments in the Hall. Again, he was nudged into the migration by others.

The cool mug of cider felt good on his hurt hand as he stood, tucked into a corner, alone in the crowd. A few sips and he'd had enough. He'd seen a route through the mob of smiling talkers.

"Hard to top it when your first role is Son of God," one loud voice declared to the young Mother.

"Daughter of God," had corrected what probably was her father. Everyone laughed.

He had set his mug on a window ledge. When he turned to go, his way was blocked by the lady in mink.

"I've been watching you. You are not who I thought." She took another deep breath. "I behaved badly," she said. "I want to apologize." Smoothing her coat, she continued, "You saved me from a painful injury. I would like to give you a Christmas gift, … if you would accept one." It seemed a concession to a decision that wasn't hers to make. "What is something you'd like this Christmas?" It was a now a directive.

The wave-off and cruel rebuke that was on his lips, waiting, disappeared as he drew breath.

    He let out a sigh and said instead, "Would you share a coffee and muffin at the coffee shop on the corner, say tomorrow about eleven? It would be a good reason for me to get out of bed."

The request had caught the lady completely off guard.

    "… if you aren't too busy," he continued.

    "… Right," she drawled cynically, and turned away at a hail from a friend.

That was why he was here, at this table in an empty coffee shop, clean-shaven, with faint hope, and hair raked into place, wondering if he should get up and get his own drink and bun. The parking lot was empty, three cars were lined up at the drive thru. The door behind him scraped, causing him to turn. Coming toward him, in a white parka with a fur-lined hood turned up and removing purple suede gloves, was the lady from last night.

She stuck out her hand assertively.

"I don't think I caught your name last night. I'm Maggie."

2

He was thunderstruck. Of all the names in the world, how could this woman have the same one as his former wife - the name she would not be called. He opened his mouth but a greeting would not come out. He was sticking out his hand in reply when he realized it was bandaged enough to look like he'd lost it.

" JJ…Jacob," he stammered and pulled it back before she crunched it.

She reached and took his hand tenderly, supporting it carefully as she looked at the bandaging.

"You get this tended at the Emergency Ward?" she asked with a laugh. It was a good icebreaker.

"It's what was around, and the kitchen drawer only had scotch tape." He waved his wound casually. That would explain the pad of Kleenex that was already fraying. "I wasn't sure you'd come," Jacob said.

She pulled out a smart phone and flashed the screen at him, "You said about eleven." She turned it back to look at it herself. The digits said it was one-minute past. Looking at the empty table, she added, "I see you've waited for me. Let's see what they offer at the counter."

"Two large coffees, one with triple milk". She turned to look at him with raised eyebrows.

"Same."

"Make it two with triple."

"In or out?" the barista asked.

"Here."

Surveying the display case, Maggie asked, "and …"

"Carrot muffin," Jacob replied. The clerk had a bag in hand and tongs in the other.

"And a Bran for me," Maggie said.

"That will be …"

That was when he realized his wallet was in the back pocket on his burned-hand side. With the bandage on his hand, he couldn't get it out.

"This is mine," said Maggie and waved her phone at the sensor.

Bleep, chirped the machine to the cash register.

"Want your receipt?" The clerk asked.

Maggie shook her head no.

Through her open coat, Jacob noticed not the blouse and slacks he had expected but a form-fitting uniform. He draped his coat over the back of his chair. He was wearing a checked flannel shirt and grey slacks with a light brown pullover sweater.

She eyed the almost match and decided not to open with the topic of wardrobe.

"I've been in the gym," Maggie explained. "Do you work out?"

Jacob laughed, "I am the original physiophobe. The further I remain from athletics, the better I like it. Had a lot of hard times in the gym as a kid. What kind of a place opens on Christmas Day for people to work out? I don't want to blunder in by mistake."

"I have my own key," she replied. "It is part of the condo complex."

They sipped and pecked at their food in silence for a few minutes before Maggie pushed at the conversational ball again.

"I watched you last night. You are not the vagrant I originally thought you might be. You probably have at least some background in the church because you were there, and you seemed to be watching the congregation rather closely as though you were cataloguing them. I'm guessing you were some sort of administrator but are retired now.

"Pretty good guessing. I used to be a church minister. That got me into counselling roles sometimes. I didn't realize I was being so obvious."

"Nobody was paying you any attention - in fact quite the opposite." Another sip. "I thought that was a life-long thing. Lose your skill at turning water into wine?"

"Actually, I passed the Post Grad. I turn it directly into Irish Whiskey." He shook his head willing the memory of the taste away.

"So, with a comeback like that, you were a bit on the liberal end of the religious spectrum. You look too young to be retired as a minister, so again I'll guess your liberal leanings got you an early exit."

"Guilty as charged."

Maggie sat back satisfied with her inquisition.

Jacob raised his mug and drained it; his serviette was empty, even of the crumbs.

"That was very nice, thank you. I don't want to hold you up from other plans. Families can be rather demanding."

"Got that right," Maggie came back. "I am the black sheep - lesbian to be specific. They could never accept that and are actually relieved if I don't show up. My tongue can get ahead of me, but in reflection, I've decided that I have too much fun tweaking their airs of pompous entitlement. It takes no more than one drink for any gathering to descend into a mutual denigration party. So, in ways you don't know, your … idea, invitation, whatever, to get together for a coffee was likely a major contribution to Peace on Earth."

"Well in any case, you have given me a gift I had not expected and which has been very pleasant. I was told as a child that on Christmas everyone should get something they needed, something they wanted, and something they didn't expect. This morning has been all three wrapped up in one." He shuffled a bit. "If you need to attend to other things in your life, you have shared more than enough of it with me to satisfy your pledge."

Maggie sighed, "Without being too pointed, this get-together isn't all about you. To use your gift groups, I'd agree this has been a pleasant time but there are still two categories not filled for me. What I really need is to see that horrible bandage you put on your hand, properly replaced. So, you will be doing me a favour by accompanying me to the Pharmacy in the high-rise over there where there are the necessities to deal with it. So, let's go, shall we?" She stood and zipped up her coat.

Jacob scrambled into his coat and hurried to catch up. He fell in step on the curb side. He thought she smiled a little when that happened.

"You live around here?" Jacob asked.

"She nodded at the Pharmacy ahead. "That's my building."

The tall tower reminded Jacob of the slab from a movie long ago. It was a bit overwhelming relative to the other buildings around it. He was also puzzled by the emphasis she placed on the description of the place they were headed, as though she owned it or something. He laughed at the thought.

Jacob wondered why a Drug Store would be open until he saw the sign bragging it was open *twenty-four-seven*.

"In my earlier life, I was Head Nurse in Surgery at our hospital," Maggie said as she passed through the door, he was holding open. She went straight to the shelves she wanted, pulled off packages and led him back to the dispensary. "I need the bandage scissors in the drawer, Andrew," she said to the clerk.

Snip. Snip. Tape was cut. He jumped when she yanked it off his skin.

"Just barely blistered," she declared as she examined his burn. "You should change this dressing at breakfast and bedtime for three days. Watch." She smeared an ointment on; it smelled antiseptic and felt cool. "Double gauze pad and secure the pad like so. This tape won't hurt your skin." Over the top she slipped a sort of a sock, open at both ends. "This protects the bandage and you can re-use it each time." More tape secured it on both ends. All the leftovers went into a bag which she thrust into his other hand. "On my tab, Andrew," directed Maggie.

"Now for my last gift from you. I want to go for a walk. Let's go down by the river." She all but turned him towards the door. "I'll meet you outside in a few minutes."

He watched her walk to the door that led into the lobby of what had to be the condo complex upstairs, waving at the concierge on duty as she punched the elevator button.

"Same to you," Jacob heard him call back.

Andrew asked if he was knew how to change the dressing.

Jacob rehearsed the steps and added, "and keep it out of the dishwater."

"Got it," said the pharmacist. He reached along the dispensary counter, pulled a bunch of plastic gloves from a box and stuffed them into Jacob's bag. "Use these if you have to wash dishes or when you shower."

Maggie joined him wearing Jeans and a black parka with reflective strips. A red toque covered her blond hair; a matching scarf peeked out at her throat. She was pulling on mittens with reflective stripes. When Jacob commented on the mitten design, she explained that she sometimes did her jogging late in the day.

"I told you I was Head Nurse in Surgery," she said as they walked along the water swishing over rocks. The paved walkway had been scraped clear. "I left the job about a year ago. Everyone was delighted to see me go because of the problem with the surgeon. He molested one of my nurses. I had him fired."

"I can't imagine what kind of effort that took," Jacob replied.

"Less than you might think, actually. The place is called 'Wellington Memorial' for a reason. My Dad endowed it."

A click happened in Jacob's brain. *Heaven's Sake. She does own the building,* he thought.

He swallowed and replied, "If your Dad is that wealthy, why were you doing nursing?"

"For something to do. And No, I did not get the job because my father bought it. In a fit of pique, I had changed my last name, about then, to my mother's maiden name. They didn't know who was behind the nameplate I wore and I earned my position on my own merits in a regular competition. They never knew who I was till Doctor What's-his-name, got too free with his hands."

They walked along quietly, appreciating the rushing of the water.

"I'm never sure what it is I like about rivers, whether it's that they drown out the sounds of daily living or that they have a sense of moving onward," Maggie observed.

"The whole water thing carries all sorts of religious baggage for me. 'Darkness was on the face of the deep' at creation, 'Water on a dry and thirsty land,' in Isaiah He had lots of water referenccs. 'Lead me beside still waters,' is in another Old Testament text you likely heard a lot. But the sound of moving water always is ironic to me - as though all the connotations that we learned and manufactured are made meaningless by water on the move. We need water but still water is not what most water is. When water moves, it reshapes things. The sermons I delivered and have heard for a lifetime always seem like pushing water uphill. That's what earned me early retirement. Amos had it when he said, 'justice should come down like an ever-flowing stream.' Well you can see how that is working these days."

Rather than follow a loop up through the residences, they opted to retrace their steps along the riverside.

By the time they were back to where they had started, Jacob had to ask, "I don't recall your mentioning why you were at church last night?"

"I live in different worlds. Doesn't everyone? That's one of mine. I guess I inherited it with the family name so force of habit took me there - that and there are a bunch of people that know me. I've been part of their financial stream for quite a while. I can count on some good groveling and unsubtle references to how short they are on their budget."

"And of course, they are nice people," Jacob added.

"And that."

The sun had slid down behind the trees on the far bank scaring a chill out of the woods. Snow-covered boulders in the stream stood out more starkly now.

"Well this has been a Christmas to remember," Jacob said. "I think I have satisfied my gifting duties as you have. I would like to thank you for making it a memorable event. I should take my leave now so as not to intrude on your kindness."

Maggie nodded, "And you are going home to watch TV or play solitaire after eating a dinner about the size of a hymnary."

Jacob looked away so she would not see his blushing, "Right except for the TV and cards. I'd probably head down to the pub. See if anyone there wants to indulge in a conversation about philosophy of the nineteenth century. Then I'll put on a few more miles to get tired enough to sleep."

"I can see what you mean about a Christmas to remember. That would be something to publish. Might rival that one last night."

"You *do* have a talent for description."

"If you'd like to join me and my other friends for dinner, I'm sure we could all scrunch over a bit to make a place."

"I probably saw enough of them last night, and they of me. That would not be a good idea."

"None of last night's crowd will be attending. This is another group I share time with. They might surprise you."

"I've had a couple rude surprises lately."

"Take a chance, Jacob."

They had walked back from the river and were passing the donut shop where they had met earlier. The sight of the empty table through the window was convincing.

"Sure. Surprise me," he said.

3

"Evening, Ms. M." greeted the concierge as they entered.

"And a lovely one to you too, Barak. This is Jacob and he's coming up to dinner with me."

The swarthy young man looked down at his computer screen and tapped a key, "Is that spelled with a 'c' or 'k'?" Jacob thought he heard the click of a camera

"A 'c' Jacob responded.

"Last name?"

"Eiger," Jacob replied.

"Good to meet you Mr. Eiger," Barak said. There was a slight nod to Maggie. "Duely noted," he continued. "You are in our guest registry."

Maggie led the way to the elevator which opened as they approached. Beside the opening, a directory of names - mostly professional offices it seemed - stopped at the fourth floor. Maggie punched the twentieth-floor button and stepped back.

"The apartments start on the eighth," Maggie explained. "We're going to the dining room on the top."

Images of a rotating upper-end, penthouse restaurant came to him - linen tablecloths, silver cutlery, tuxedo'd staff bending stiffly, popped to mind. Jacob suddenly felt under dressed.

"I didn't bring a tie," he said.

"You'll be alright."

As Jacob was reflecting on the 'surprise' that might await him at dinner, the elevator door announced the floor and opened into a dim space and onto nothing he had imagined.

The panoramic view through floor-to-ceiling windows was arresting. The stream rushed by at their feet, the woodland beyond and then farmland to the west was obliquely lit by moonlight and a starry spread of sky. *Wow* was all Jacob could say, but that was only the start.

His eye followed the windows around; his ears invited them towards the cheerful chattering of children's voices; the delicious smells drew him around the elevator bank into a brightly lit room filled with people and tables and a cafeteria at the far end.

The room was an interior designer's masterpiece. Comfortable chairs clustered in sitting arrangements in out-of-the-way spaces; interesting sculptures peeked around posts; stunning huge photographs of people from around the world smiled back from interior walls; real plants, strategically placed, glowed from careful attention.

A United Nations of racial mixes was concentrated at the distant end of the space around tables and everyone there seemed to be smiling also - well except for the toddler who seemed lost. While Jacob watched, a stranger scooped up the disoriented child and delivered her to her Mother who had just returned to a table with plates of food.

"Good Heavens," Jacob blurted. "They're all women!"

Maggie just laughed, "Hang your coat here." She took off hers by example. When he saw her flannel check beneath, he didn't feel so badly about his. "I see a table we could join," she said.

As they threaded their way through the crowd, his eyes never stopped jumping one way and the other. By the time they had arrived at their table, he had confirmed that aside from children, he was the only adult male in the room. There were some teens and young adults, but he was the only male that could be called a senior.

The table was wooden with live edges. It gleamed between the plates, cups, and cutlery on it. Swirls of annual rings and knots hinted at patterns that would please the eye and intrigue the mind after the implements were gone.

"May we join you, Tina?" Maggie asked.

"Of course! Slide your chair over, Sarah. And move Celly as well." Celly was in a highchair. Maggie made for the place opened for her and Jacob was gestured to the place beside the boy. "This is Brian," Tina said.

"This is Jacob," Maggie said to all. "He's a visitor." And then to her guest, Maggie said, "We should get our dinner."

Jacob fell in line and returned with a bowl filled with bowtie pasta and veggies in an aromatic sauce along with three thick slices of multigrain bread and butter to match. He saw only fruit for dessert and picked up an apple. He was directed to the coffee/tea table if he wanted it then.

He buttered his bread under the silent but laser gaze of Celly across the table.

"How old are you?" asked Brian.

"How old do you think?"

"A hundred," declared the child.

"You're absolutely right," Jacob replied, "just last summer. What gave me away?"

"You have grey hair."

"That will do it every time. How old are you?"

"I'm six and a half."

"So, your birthday must be next summer also. What day?"

The child rhymed off the date slowly, looking to mother. He managed, without prompts. Jacob managed to get a bite of his food. It was delicious.

"Well, that is a most remarkable co-incidence," Jacob said. "That is my birthday too. What do you do for a party?"

While the child recited the names of his many friends who would gather and the favourite games they would play, Jacob finished his bowl and cleaned it with his last crust. Celly's eyes never left him.

"What do you do on your birthday?" Brian asked.

"I celebrate being well and happy to see the sun,"

"Do you have friends?"

"Not around here."

"You could be my friend," Brian offered,

"and you could come to my party. We could have our parties together."

"That sounds like a wonderful idea."

Throughout the conversation, Tina and Maggie had remained quiet watching the interchange. Celly just looked at him steadily. Even when Sarah spooned the last bites of her food into her, she did not take her eyes off the man across the table.

All the children watched as he sliced his apple into thin slices and notched out the core in each piece.

"I can't eat apples," volunteered Brain. "I lost my front teeth." He displayed a toothless grin.

"Without those front ones, it is hard to bite an apple. Would you like to help me eat mine? You can crunch up a piece with your back teeth."

The child accepted the sliver, after receiving a nod from Mom, and then a second slightly thicker one and managed to get both chewed up and swallowed.

There seemed to be a communal rustle. Most families were finished and bedtime would likely be the next item on the agenda. As they left, single women of various ages grouped with fresh coffee. Maggie made no attempt to join them bringing him a well-milked coffee to their table instead. With Brian gone, he could admire the lights twinkling below. The moon was headed for the horizon.

"Well you had that right," Jacob said. "In my wildest dreams, I never thought of this scene when I thought of Christmas Dinner. Tell me about it."

"This is a women's community. There is only one rule and it is that each must give and receive respect with grace. Every woman here has a terrible story of abuse to tell. This is their sanctuary. That's why we're here and they are over there." She glanced past his shoulder. He didn't need to turn around. "Some are still really uneasy about the presence of a man in their midst."

"And that would explain Celly's attentive interest."

"*That* and being almost two years old."

"Because of my wealthy parents, I inherited enough money to play God. Because of father's architectural contacts at the hospital, I had access to an imaginative group of engineers and architects who could design a place like this. From my nursing background, I have a lot of community contacts that have found these people. So here the building is and we are. Each person receives the usual financial support from the government and they all have subsidized housing on the floors below. We have offices for all the needed social and professional services downstairs in this building. Nobody needs to travel anywhere to access them. The condo corporation has also organized employment training in the various offices downstairs or in our food-growing operation. Children go to school on the fifth to seventh floors so they and their mothers are secure. That's another fear of many - that their abusive relatives will attempt to kidnap them.

"Can't the other parent just walk into the school and pick up the kid?" Jacob asked returning to the young ones.

"Access is only by elevator and nobody gets out of that box that we don't recognize or on a floor we don't approve. We simply shuffle unwelcome visitors back to the lobby and explain the system must be out of order. If they try again, they get routed to the parking garage where police park their vehicles. The Community Police Office is in the commercial suite as well.

"Fire escapes?"

"Well secured and monitored. Exit only - no re-entry on another floor"

She nodded to the young adults who had formed their own group in a far corner, "When our students graduate, they go to colleges and universities. You see some of them who've returned home for the season."

"Every woman here works in some capacity for the good of their community. Every office in the commercial complex is obliged to train and hire women who live here. We make their rents attractive to do so. To maintain the reliable, competent, and flexible labour pool, we encourage them to share a portion of their profits with the training and housing program. We have every profession," she paused to reword her statement, "but the oldest one," she added, "so our graduates are well-skilled and financially secure to make their own way when they leave us.

"I didn't see any Christmas stuff up anywhere."

"All religions must be left at the door. Respect may be a tenet of religious communities but it usually works for those at the top. They get, those below, give. It's one of the reasons we revert to that elemental, prehistoric need to be acknowledged gratefully. Rather than try to cater to all religions we ignore them all." She paused to scan the room then returned her gaze, with steady purpose, to him.

"All religions act, intentionally or otherwise, at separating or stigmatizing others. They are the profanity they seek to condemn. 'Sanctify' means 'to set apart'. We are not served by such isolation within them. We can thrive and find joy in the celebration of our humanity, not our contrived differences. So, religion stops at the lobby. I got the feeling during the day, that you would probably see our point, even if you don't agree with it."

Jacob squinted while he tried to compose a reply, "You can do no right here, I fear. In the eyes of those who would oppose you, will be listed the entry requirements. It's a Charter Right to freely express religion. Another arrow in their quiver is that you abuse power when you ask a desperate woman to sell her soul and those of her children, in exchange for sanctuary."

"Well I'm not the one who decided the rules. The group did that, and they protect themselves by saying this collective is a private club, an offshoot, open to all who espouse this religion of humanity. The God you and your ilk created is a vindictive male chauvinist and deserves to be dethroned."

"As long as you are female."

"For now. There is space across the parking lot for a future companion building for similarly abused or isolated men."

"So, your members have to join a new religion and renounce their old one, to remain. Seems circuitous to have to do that, even ironic."

"Only game in town."

"Though it contradicts every oath I ever had to take, you are demonstrating exactly where my thoughts took me when I was booted out of the sacred halls I used to inhabit. In fact, any study of the historical Jesus, as a person, would lead me to the conclusion that he would bless your initiative more than the Churches that claim him. He was the one that kept tossing up alternatives to the Empire. That's what you have done here. You'd have him doubled up laughing downstairs, and finding he was not allowed up here because he's a man, would have him rolling on the floor. Truly, that is really funny."

Jacob looked at his cold empty cup, "It is past my bedtime. I should be going."

"I'll take you down."

As they stepped into the lobby, Jacob asked, "If you need a lecturer in Classical to Modern Philosophy, Critical Thinking Skills and Rhetoric, or the study of Greek or Latin, I'd be pleased to offer what I can. They are all necessary talents to anyone who would enter political life and I can't think how anyone from your community could avoid finding themselves on such a road."

Maggie handed him a card, "This is how to contact me." Then she handed him a second card and pen. "Would you share your contacts?"

He did.

4

"You are cleared to come to the School on levels five and six only and the cafeteria on the top floor," explained the principal handing over an identity card. Scan this as you enter and punch the right buttons. Maggie had already explained the major part of his job as a counsellor after he had presented his credentials. The classroom gig rounded out his time and justified the salary he was now being paid. "Your classroom is number 8 down this hall. If you would like to join the students in games in the gym or jogging or the fitness rooms, you'd be welcome. There are change rooms at the elevator."

"I noticed them."

"We encourage a personal connection that extends beyond your subject area. We hope you will take advantage of that. We find sharing exercise options extends the knowledge into daily life by getting it out of the textbook."

He was about to proclaim his aversion to things athletic but caught the words in time, "Is it permitted to walk on the jogging track? It's the one around the building on the balcony outside is it not?"

"Correct and we follow the rules of the road - slower traffic keeps right."

"How big is the class I teach?" Jacob asked.

"There are twenty-two students - from age six to sixteen."

Jacob had been thinking there might be single digits, "That seems large."

"You will find the older ones help the younger ones as a demonstration of our efforts to show respect for all."

I guess that sinks the library of texts, I have, he thought.

"Is there a course of Study?"

"We're counting on you to build one that might be called 'Critical Thinking', that will prepare students for the world they face. There is no such course from the Provincial Ministry of Education, so you have a fair amount of latitude. Just don't waste their time."

The last statement caught Jacob's full attention and he looked back at the steel stare that held him.

"I am looking forward to the challenge. In my previous job, teaching anyone was not the point of our time together, unless you consider rote learning the aim. How long are the periods?"

"Forty minutes."

"When do classes start?"

"Your class is in the gym right now. You can collect them there and take them to your classroom. There is about half an hour left in the period."

The gym was three floors high. A gallery of seats was about halfway up the wall and occupied two sides of the space. A climbing wall, the top of which was accessed from the gallery, allowed for safety stations to secure those trying to make their way up. Every climber was on a safety rope and they were held by a fellow, anchored at the top. As soon as he appeared in the gym with the Principal, he was noticed. Quickly climbing, shooting hoops, tumbling, and hopscotch all came to a halt.

When they had all grouped and were obviously ready to head down the hall, Jacob asked, "Would you object if we just stayed here for the time remaining in our period? Maybe we could do anything necessary for our first gathering right here."

He looked around the crescent of faces. All nodded. They sat where they stood; one brought a large exercise ball for him to sit on. *Was this a test to see if he could sit on it?* he wondered.

"Maybe we could start with names," he invited once he got used to the bouncy seat. "My name is," he was about to say 'Reverend', but caught himself in time. "Jacob Eiger, I really like thinking about … whatever and that is why I'm here. Your Principal asked me to teach you about different ways to think about things."

"Could you tell me your name and something you like to do?" He looked to the child in front of him. "I'll try to remember your names but please help me remember until I get used to you. There are more of you than of me." It caused a ripple of snickers through the group.

Each of the children gave his or her name and something they liked to do. Jacob was glad when the younger ones went on at length and began to add a list of friends and events. It gave him time to write the names down and review them as he summarized such epistles. He was a bit surprised at the length to which even the smallest spoke and the confidence in their voices but he did have to remind them there was only about a minute for each person before the change of period. With minutes left, he asked each for the most important problem they were currently addressing. He wrote them down too before they all moved off.

5

Jacob looked as his notes as he addressed the class, lined up at desks in his classroom.

"I can see from the list of problems you are dealing with, that almost every topic you mention could be addressed with a pattern that has served humans around the world for a long time. That is my specialty - outlining a pattern that has served centuries of people in their search for answers to questions. Sometimes those searchers came to conclusions that were not appreciated by others around them which led to some really hard choices. Do you abandon where the search has led and keep your job, or even your life, or do you follow the quest and become isolated, desperately poor, even executed?" He looked around at the intent faces.

"I'm being dramatic to get your attention," Jacob confessed and stepped back and sat down so he was at their level. "Almost all problems are not life-threatening but they provide a place to apply the pattern of solving that will serve you well in more serious decisions. So, before you can apply a pattern of problem solving, you need a problem and the problem will arise because of your value system. You need to know what is most important to you."

The kids were starting to fidget.

"We're going to work backwards on the value system. I'm going to start with the problem and you're going to tell me what it says is valuable to the person who claimed it. Let me start with …" he looked at his notes again. "Let me talk about Broccoli. Brian doesn't like Broccoli and his problem is that he has to eat it to make his mother happy. So, what values does Brian hold?"

"Pleasing himself," said one of the senior students.

"Obeying authority," said another.

"Obeying the group standard that put the broccoli on the table," corrected another. "They thought it was OK or it wouldn't have appeared. So, there is a bunch of people who thought there was something good about broccoli."

Brian's head, and those of his age group were swiveling like casters as the older kids kept butting in. Jacob held up a hand to stop the discussion and give the problem back to Brian.

"Brian? What do you think?"

"I just want to have dessert and Mom says I can't till I eat my broccoli," he asserted.

"So just eat it," said the senior student."

"But I don't like it. It tastes terrible. It makes me feel sick."

"Do you think Brian could be right?" Jacob asked. "Could Broccoli really make Brian sick?"

"Well he did eat it and he didn't throw up," said one of the older girls, "so maybe he's just playing a game?'

Another girl broke in, "I didn't throw up but bread used to give me an awful gut ache. The doctor said I'm gluten intolerant. It could be something like that for Brian. Maybe he has something we don't have but it makes broccoli bad for him."

Jacob jumped in, "Anya has made an important point that we need to return to. I don't want to lose track of it so I'm going to write it down on the board." He stepped to the Board and wrote about the middle of the space and about halfway down at one end:

"Is good for some,
good for all?"

"I want you to write that down under these other headings in your notebooks."

He turned back to the board and wrote at the top of the slate in the center, "VALUE SYSTEM" and then under it on the left, he wrote "lead to PROBLEMS" and under that "SOLUTIONS" The word "PROBLEMS" lined up with his question on the right that was separated by a space. "SOLUTIONS" was under the question.

"This will be a foundation theme for our course," Jacob stressed. "I will bring it up again and again. You will get tired of hearing me say it but remembering it will serve you well. So, let's talk about solutions that Brian might consider as he deals with this dilemma." The students obediently copied the material on the board into their workbooks.

As they did, he asked one of the older students who hadn't contributed, and had already finished copying, "Would you like to write down the suggested solutions when everyone starts to offer them?" The student stood obediently and took the chalk. "It's Phillip, is it not?"

The student nodded.

"Hold it this way," Jacob indicated demonstrating how to hold it pinched by his thumb against all four fingertips, "so it doesn't squeak."

When the suggestions started coming, Phillip wrote them down the right margin of the board where Jacob had directed. Not being used to the new medium, it took a while. He also misspelled several words but nobody corrected him.

"Hold your nose when you swallow it," said one child.

"Slide it onto your sister's plate when your Mom is looking away."

"Sprinkle it with Salt."

"Put sugar on it."

"Give up dessert."

"Ask for an alternate before it gets on your plate."

"Ask for an allergy test."

When they ran out of space on the board, Jacob halted the process and then took back the chalk.

He circled the alternatives and then to the left, he wrote in large capitals "CHOICES" as he asked, "so which of the solutions is the answer for you Brian?"

The word centered on the right edge of the board. With big heavy lines, Jacob connected the capitalized words and they framed, in a diamond pattern, the question he'd started out with.

"So that's what we will be talking about for the whole course. Values beget Problems. Problems demand Solutions. Solutions offer Choices. Choices require Values." With each point Jacob punched the board with the chalk and splinters flew. "And at every corner, the question of who the decisions should apply to will arise. Make that box in your notebooks. Any questions?"

"Brian," called a classmate. Brian looked up from his copying when his name was called. "Are you going to eat your broccoli next time?"

Everyone, especially Brian, laughed.

6

"Does anyone know how this building is heated?" asked Jacob to begin a lesson long after the Solstice celebrations had been compared in the various cultures represented in their community. Actually, he'd run out of ideas but bumping into the stationary engineer in the elevator had given him what he was working on at the moment.

Blank stares and silence met his question.

"Well think about it. All winter long we've looked out on the snowy fields around here. Do you recall the storm that shut down all the streets because of snowdrifts? We watched them from those windows right out there."

He pointed through the window wall of his classroom to a similar outside wall on the other side of the corridor. On days when he knew his lesson would be a challenge, he always interspersed his teaching in ten-minute talks with sprints around the circuit corridor that surrounded the building on each floor.

"Remember how cold they said it was. Wind chills of minus thirty Celsius. We talked about what that meant, who Celsius was. And yet we had no coats. We stood there and blew our breath onto the window."

"The window was so cold," said one child

"You said that what made out breath mist on the window was one of the processes that made the snow clouds," said another.

Jacob nodded to each reply.

"And yet we stood there in comfortable warmth and we never even thought about it, never questioned why we were warm. That is another aspect of philosophy. We often ask questions that most people do not. That's for another day. What I want to do today is to have someone who knows why and how this building stays warm, tell you about that because that whole machinery is at the root of our famous Square. He drew it hastily on the board but only put letters at the corners. The students told him what the words were.

"What we are looking at today is a solution." He tapped the 'S' with his chalk. "The Problem we are addressing is 'How to keep the building, and ourselves, warm'." He wrote the words under the 'P'. "At the end of the presentation, we'll talk about 'Values' and 'Choices' that are demonstrated by using this process."

He scanned the group, "So, is everyone clear that the task today is three-fold? You need to know," and he wrote on the board as he spoke. "1) how the building is heated, 2) what choices were made in using this process, 3) what values were shown by the builders."

Immediately the children picked up pens to write the three lines he'd written.

"Stop," he directed. "Put each of these statements at the top of separate pages."

As they wrote the classroom door opened and a plainly dressed person dressed in overalls, long hair tightly tied back, entered. Jacob just waved her to the front of the room and spread his hands to signal she could begin.

Asa was not a handsome woman by any standard but spirit. She'd been scarred badly before she escaped the community that assumed violence towards women was normal, even expected. She'd managed, through hard work, to become a skilled manager of the systems that kept this building running smoothly and made it a showcase. To get to this point, she'd done a lot of things she did not want to talk about. But now with this success in her hands she thought she'd kill anyone who would try to take it from her. For the first time in her life, she was valued for her skill, inventiveness and dedication and nobody knew this place like she did.

"I'm Asa," she said softly, "and Mr. Eiger asked me to tell you how this building stays warm. That is the most favourite thing I know to talk about. But sometimes

I might tell you things in the wrong order and just confuse you. Please tell me, right away, if I mixed you up. I want you to love this building like I do. It is the most amazing place in the world." A pin drop could be heard.

"We warm the building by blowing warm air around the place. It comes into every room and hall through those grills in the ceiling." She pointed up. Some looked following her finger; some wrote in their notebooks. "It is where we get the heat to make the air warm, that is so special about this place. We do not get it from burning oil or gas in a giant fireplace in the basement. We get it from the sun." She looked up and raised her hands to the ceiling and her face shone as though it was sunlit - the priestess in her temple.

"You know how all the rooms are in the middle of this building and around each floor is a hallway on the outside." Every child nodded.

"In the winter, that space insulates and protects the inner rooms. We leave it cool but not cold. When the sun shines into that space, in summer, it can get quite warm. What we do is suck up that warm air and replace it with cool air in the summer. In the winter, the air would be cold if we didn't draw that air out and replace it with warm. So, you can see that two different things happen depending on the time of year. Right now, we want to warm that space because it is so cold so we have to warm the air that comes to the halls with the heat of last summer's sun. We collected that heat back then and we've put it in gigantic, insulated pools under the building. The stuff in there is so hot it is like lava from a volcano. It is not lava but a salt, like table salt, that is so hot it has melted and looks like gravy.

"Do you mean the salt is dissolved?" asked an older boy.

"No, the salt has melted like you can melt sugar or candle wax, or ice. It takes heat energy to make those things change to liquids. If you keep them liquid, they hold onto the energy that it took to make them that way. If you want the heat back, let the material cool. When it goes through the change back to a solid, it has to release the heat it held. If you blow air over it at just that time, the heat goes into the air and you can blow that warmed air into this classroom or anywhere else to make it warm."

"Lava would have a lot of heat in it. How do you get only the right amount of heat out? If you got out too much could the building catch fire?" asked one of the senior girls

"Yes. If it were uncontrolled, this building could burn up. So, we control the process with ruthless care. It takes years to learn how to do that but it is a job any one of you could do." She pulled up her sleeve to show burn scars. "This happened to me when I was a child and too much of a scalding substance cooled on my skin and cooked it. She did not point to her neck and cheek but the children glanced at her face and back. The tone of her voice could cut steel.

After a breath, she smiled and her mellow sound returned, "We extract the heat a bit at a time, in steps though what we call heat exchangers. The special liquid goes through pipes in the molten salt and comes out hot. The melted salt is slightly cooler. That really hot special liquid transfers the heat to another liquid in another exchanger. After several such exchanges we have manageable amounts of heat to warm this building, the greenhouse area." She reviewed the steps walking across the room to new places for each exchanger.

"We can also use the heat to boil water and make steam that we blast at a propellor on a generator. It turns the generator and make electricity." She pulled a collection of pinwheels from a bag she'd set beside her and handed them to outstretched hands in front of her. The children blew on them of course and waved them around.

Over the chatter of small voices, a senior asked, "Can electricity go backwards?" He waved at the pinwheels. "If those wheels were folded the other way, they would rotate the other way? Would the electricity from such a generator be different from one with vanes folded like those?" He waved at the toys.

"The short answer is there is one kind of electricity, but in the case you mention, it could be out of phase with the other and so 'cancel' it out in a spectacular spark. What is also possible is to change the generator details so that it would be compatible." As she spoke, she moved through the room and collected the pinwheels.

"Besides last summer's sun, there are two other sources of heat we use in this building. I'll save the best one till last by telling you how you children and everybody in this building, all the lights and heat from the kitchen all gets collected every minute. The air that comes from here is collected through those grills there," she pointed to a second set in the wall, "and taken to a heat exchanger where the heat is harvested. You know how you are all hotter than that desk or the floor don't you." They all agreed.

"Well these inside walls are so well insulated that if we harvest all the body heat from all the people in the building, and all the lights and all the computers and machines working in this place, we can almost balance what we need. The warmth can go back to a room supply or be stored by melting the salt again." The children had forgotten to write what they were listening intently.

"Now the problem is that moving that air about takes big fans and those big fans take electricity and that is where the best of our heating systems comes in. On the roof of this building facing upward to the sky is a collection of mirrors that focus the summer sun onto a ball that gets as hot as a rocket engine's exhaust. You've started fires with a magnifying glass?" A few had.

"You who have, tell the others. We focus that energy onto the ball and collect it to feed the molten salt store AND to feed the steam generators that spin the turbines. The electricity we generate with that collector is what pays for this building and all the needs of us within it. We could be 'off grid' as they say except, we'd have too much electricity. We have to be 'on-grid' to get rid of what we have in excess. Electricity, is for us, a waste product."

"Now before we end, I want to show you the sort of gadgets we use to turn on the fans or pumps to heat and cool things." She pulled out different thermostats from her bottomless bag. "When you warm the sensor of these devices something changes." She showed how the metal strip bent with the heat from a hair dryer, or the mercury rose in the tube. "As the mercury goes up, the laser beam is broken and the switch turns off. See that?" She showed a couple more times. "And then one bends and breaks contact as it gets warm, then when it cools, it bends back and makes contact again so the motor would come on. So, we have loads of these monitoring and controlling all our heating systems. Here you play with them." She set them down and stepped back. "Here are more," she said as she went to the back of the room where those furthest away were feeling sad about being shut out.

*

As Asa spoke, and drew the children more and more deeply into her work, Jacob sat at the back watching and slowly slipping into the comparison with his own life. Like her, he had been injured; unlike her, his injuries didn't show outside - well he thought he appeared unscarred. Like her, he had escaped a life of stultifying oppression; unlike her he had not grasped the true power of his new connections. Like her had been excited by the community in which he now found himself; unlike her, he was the wrong gender to be accepted unconditionally within this sanctuary of social wrecks.

He'd felt ill prepared to raise children when age and family expectation dictated, he should be married. That turned out well enough though. His wife and he had not been 'blessed with children', as his congregants would have said. Technical solutions were just not part of the family process of the community so they remained onlookers to the childrearing practices around them. The community had urged, then supported, his move into the ministry. That's where he found his first real bind. He found himself crediting an inscrutable and infallible deity when he was called upon to advise on disciplining children by hauling out adages like 'sparing the rod would spoil the child'. It was a crack that only grew with time.

As counterpoint to his public persona, he and his wife led a subversive life. They were secret questioners of the whole religious existence they had to lead. The first sabbatical was a masterpiece of deceptively coordinated enrolment in programs of forbidden philosophies and religions behind a syllabus of approved classes. The experience only raised more questions. Strike one.

They returned refreshed to their isolation and to 'worship' of the vengeful and chauvinistic deity he was expected to proclaim. Another chance arose to repeat the research into the history of philosophical thought and again they used their well-oiled skills to hide what they really were studying. They returned even further frustrated. Strike two. Then it was back for the countdown to retirement. When Margaret died, that was strike three. His torrent of revelations burst on his stunned congregation and he was out.

He took an early pension and occasional pulpit coverage for holidays or illness in liberal communities to live on. With the charity of friends who needed their houses cared for while they studied abroad, it was enough. His new position as a teacher of philosophy, to children who couldn't spell the word, was a thrilling turn for him. It opened to him vistas he had yearned to explore after reading the brochures with his wife, in secret, for years. In place of the certainty and absolute authority of his previous life, he basked in the ability to question everything. He'd never felt so liberated. He was dizzy with delight; he couldn't stop laughing at the thrill of discovery. Every new revelation he enjoyed was a moment to share with his wife's memory. How she would have loved to do this. How her death seemed more and more like the ultimate sacrifice through which he had been set free.

The period was ending. The children returned the equipment and were gone. Asa sat slowly into a chair and sighed. She was not comfortable being on center stage.

"You are an inspiration," Jacob said, from the back of the room. "You had everyone's attention and I'm sure there will be a lineup at your door for their practice program when they are able to do it. I'd figured out the heat capture of the architecture but the mirrors on the roof was a surprise."

"We got a grant under a Federal program to build it and try it out. It hardly justifies itself during the winter but in summer it works overtime. So, we are self-sustaining because of it."

It is not just the details you talked about; it is the way you do it. The passion that shines out of your words is wonderful to hear and see. You've given me a new way to think about this place - it's almost like being inside an act of worship. I feel humbled and awed. Thank you."

Asa looked at her hands in embarrassment, "I should be going. Thank you for the chance to share what I do." She scooped up her bag and was about to scurry out but she stopped. "Thank you for your invitation. It brought me out of a comfortable but small place. It was hard but I'm glad you asked me." Jacob nodded in reply.

Rarely had Jacob received such a comment. His reply escaped him before he thought about it. "I think we are all called to do just that, encourage every small step of success, rejoice in accomplishment," he said.

7

The semester worked its way towards the Spring Equinox. Nobody mentioned Easter. There were no bunnies or eggs to be hunted for. The custom was mentioned in passing at a dinner as though it belonged to a primitive species of the past when chocolate was passed about to everyone. New clothes were a matter of need for growing bodies or because of weather conditions. Maybe they were worn beyond repair. Style and fashion rested on function first, but any garment came in different colours. Some found ways to wear their garments in eye-catching, creative ways - scarves became wrist-wraps; socks stuffed and sewn to headbands made interesting hats.

Jacob was forced, by the various ethnic backgrounds in the community, to search out the wisdom teachers and philosophers from around the world. It was so easy to start with the 'list of sayings' from any source and simply ask how that list got across the time span between origin and now.

The children jumped at his questions. "The person told his family and they told others." So, the failings of oral tradition were explored with the Memory Game.

"They wrote the sayings down," said one student with a condescending sigh. That led to a comparison of their notes of the lecture Asa delivered about the building heating system.

"And in those days, not everyone could write," Jacob added. "It was not a highly prized skill if the snide comments that survive about scribes of the period are to be believed. It seems like it might have been maybe like speaking a language nobody else knew when you were at a party - rather rude. And it could have been derided as evidence of a lack of memory skill. Could you not remember what the story was? What was the need to write it down? Look at the time and effort that went into making something to write on, the paper or clay tablet, the ink or stylus. And where do you put such stuff? If you lose those records, are they gone because you counted on them instead of just remembering? Well those with memory of the event can come to the rescue, so what was the point in writing it down in the first place?

"The writers had a couple of comeback arguments. First everyone could give examples of people recalling a single event differently and the students could offer examples. acob even had a recording of a favourite song from a distant Musical to play in which two seniors, with the wisdom of years, described their first meeting. The song is called "I remember it well," he said as he cued and ran it.

"The second supporting argument, and this was a big one, was that a writer could send a message or recollection to someone far away without going there personally. In a time of empire and trade, that was a clincher."

"That reason was quickly expanded into yet another strength. Writing allowed you to communicate through time as well as space. People who were not born, if they had the skill, could read of events that happened to ancient forbearers. Now that carried a mystical quality with it. Imagine communing with a spirit from the past and telling a story or a significant event and what the elder thought it meant. I mean that almost sounds spooky." Some of the children chattered nervously.

"So, scribes carried some suspicious baggage that is largely forgotten now," Jacob concluded.

"But the writers won, didn't they," said one of the older students.

"They did," Jacob agreed, "But not completely. All the problems of the origin still are with us. Who wrote it? What did the writer see or miss? Did they make up events to make a point?" He wrote each point on the board. "And then there are the copiers. What layers of errors, deletions or additions came with each new copy? This is one of my favourite examples."

He pulled up pictures of The Book of Kells, "This is a manuscript copied by scribes about fifteen hundred years ago. It was supposed to be a copy of four gospels of the Christian New Testament - a holy book. Aside from it being a masterpiece of miniature detail, the scribes made errors that the others on the team caught. Oops!" He showed words that had been repeated and the code symbols that directed the reader to ignore those duplicated parts.

"There is another unwritten secret in the imagery used also. Surrounding the text are borders of interleaved lines that all link. The tradition into which this scripture was brought had a whole different understanding of life. To the ancients, life and death was a circle, and that belief was conveyed in the patterns of the border. The Christian philosophy was that life ended in death - it was a line, not a circle. So, this Book became a compromise. The linear philosophy was surrounded by, enclosed within, the circles of the earlier culture. These millennia later it is the artistic values that are revered. Few people can read the words on the page. The arguments over what those words mean can be seen in the following." He pulled up a screen listing the multiple versions in print, of the original bible.

"So, we can conclude that no ancient saying of wisdom or wonder has survived intact to reach us today through any process of translation or copying. All have suffered the changes of time and that is why we are called to ask questions of everything you are asked to believe." He tapped the diamond-shaped figure with the letters that had permanent residence in the upper corner of the board. "That is why we do this. That is what education is about and for - so that you can evaluate and select the helpful wisdom of the past or use it to make up your own.

He thought he might have slipped into his sermon mode judging from the blank faces of many. It was Brian who saved the day.

"The people who made the border of the Kells Book used that same diamond-shape sir. They turned it to make it look like a box and sometimes the diamonds seem to weave together. Was that another message they were sneaking in?"

Jacob looked at the image of the Man, Lion, Bull and Eagle that Brian was pointing to with new eyes and laughed, "You may very well be right," and he pointed to the figures for the rest of the class. "Brian, you are so sharp. Give that man a gold star!"

*

When the fire bell rang Jacob was in the lounge on the top floor reading in preparation for a future class. He noticed there seemed to be a large number of students in the space but he hadn't been there enough to be an authority on student after-class practice. It seemed strange for such a nice day anyway. *They are usually playing outside,* he thought. Maybe it was a special dinner menu. He went back to his book.

The required semi-annual Fire Drill had been well broadcast in the notes of the day. He'd just forgotten about it when it went off. He got up from his book and made for the stairwell, also forgetting he was on the twentieth story. He found himself alone at the fire door.

Looking back, only a few remained standing at the four posts in short queues. One of his students, Kyle, beckoned him back. With the clanging getting really annoying, Jacob came back to see the lead mother in the line step, with her young child, into the doorway that opened in the post. He had thought it was a supporting structure. He looked around. Maybe ten people were at the other posts.

"No," Kyle said to him in reply to the confused look on his face, "Not the stairs. This is a safety chute. Sort of like the airplane escape things that pop out of the side of the airplane if it has an emergency landing."

The teen ahead moved up to the door when it opened again a few seconds later. "No. I'll go with Jacob," he shouted over the bell to the invitation to share the descent. "This is your first time isn't it?" he asked looking at Jacob. Jacob nodded still puzzled.

The door closed and there was a swishing sound. Kyle was about to explain some details when the door opened again. Kyle stepped forward, steering Jacob ahead of him, into a cylindrical enclosure about the size of an old-fashioned phone booth.

"Stay away from the side," Kyle directed. "Hands on my shoulders." With that, the kid grabbed Jacob's hips. "Yawn. Open your mouth and yawn," he repeated.

"It drops fast at the start." The words were not out of his mouth and Jacob was opening his mouth when Jacob's stomach shot up into his throat.

It felt almost like a free-fall that dropped and dropped then gradually slowed. The side of the tube opened and Kyle spun Jacob gently but quickly pushed him out into a ground-floor lobby filled with chattering, smiling people. The door clacked closed behind them.

"Holy Smoke! What was that?"

"Fun eh?"

Jacob was still unnerved. A new arrival, the person behind them upstairs, stepped nimbly from the open door and it closed again.

With teen-age nonchalance Kyle explained. "There is a deck of trays beside these tubes on each floor," he explained. "When the fire bell sounds, the lowest snaps into the tube and becomes a floor and the door opens for the first escapee. You step in, punch the button and it drops on a cushion of air that compresses as you get down until it is enough to balance your weight and stop us at the bottom."

"And if there is a leak?"

"Never happened. There are emergency cylinders of compressed gas that will open if there is too much weight or the electronics fail. So, look at the stop clock up there. Three minutes to evacuate our floor and that will be the last coming down the stairs from the offices on the lower floors. If we'd taken the stairs, we'd still be in transit, assuming nobody fell, or that we didn't run into smoke on lower levels. We really like fire drills. That's why there were so many in the lounge before."

"You have to open your mouth because of the pressure changes. It can even handle people in wheelchairs. If their device is too big, we put a chair in the space and move them to that. We'd never get a wheelchair down from there. And no ladder would make it up. Neat eh?"

Maggie appeared in the crowd doing a head count, "Isn't that fun?"

"Rhetorical question," Jacob replied as his pulse slowed.

She smiled and raised her voice to direct everyone to exit into the main lobby and use the elevators to the cafeteria for dinner in half an hour. A few of the teens challenged each other to run up the stairs.

"You can't get out of the stairwell onto a floor," Maggie said. "Only exit is on this level."

"Could we send someone up to open the door at the top?"

"Well maybe this once," she laughed. The kids organized it. One was appointed timekeeper to start them at intervals. It was only to be a survival test, not speed.

Everyone who started, just wanted to finish. Jacob noticed some of the older ones accompanied the younger ones as buddies. It was simply assumed everyone would have a helper if they needed it.

The mob did not clear into the elevator lobby as Maggie expected. Almost immediately her communicator buzzed at her belt. She snapped it open and immediately her face went hard.

"Back this way everybody. Exit the building this way quickly. It is an emergency. Quickly, Quickly." She turned people that had been headed into the lobby around and nudged them towards the exterior doors. "Hold the doors open,"

"Quickly," she shouted again. "Exit this way now. Faster." The urgency in her voice started to move the crowd from a shamble into a quickstep.

"Jacob. Shout up the stairwell and call the children back. There are twelve of them."

Jacob shouted and got complaining replies. He urged careful speed as Maggie had. "It's harder coming down than you think. Don't fall. Hold the railing but come fast. There is an emergency."

With everyone milling about in the cool spring air outside wanting to know what had happened, the approaching sirens seemed to confirm something indeed was wrong.

Maggie assigned a parent who was also a teacher to do a count and headed immediately back into the building.

"Come along," she summoned to Jacob. He followed her through into the elevator lobby vacant now, except for Barak.

Police and vehicles could be seen through the glass front arrayed like a barricade. Barak was pointing to the open elevator door and through it, against the wall of the elevator car, the bulging black briefcase.

Maggie turned back to Barak. "I called the downstairs community Police Office when I saw it after the Fire Drill and turned on the closed-circuit feed to them so they could see it. They called in the emergency," he said. "They called it a possible bomb."

*

"I think I need to explain about the scare after the Fire Drill," Maggie said to everyone in the dining room after a delayed meal. She explained why the police, fire, and ambulance vehicles had arrived and why they left so quickly.

"A briefcase was left in the elevator during the drill. Because of earlier threats against our residents, we are on a police watch list. The possibility of a bomb was what brought all the emergency teams. I've expressed our thanks for such prompt reaction. The professional who occupies one of our lower-floor offices, left the case. They returned to collect it when they got home and found they'd forgotten it because of the many other files they were carrying and dropped in the process.

There was widespread laughter. Maggie allowed it to go on along with the speculation about who it was, then she raised her hand for silence, "We cannot ignore the continuing threat to our place here. Many of you still wrestle against the effects of the violence that drove you here. Let me use the chance to remind you, one and all, that we have procedures that are instantly ready to act if you feel threatened. We all need to be prepared should old scores seek to be settled. You all remember the elevator signal should you feel in danger."

Children jumped enthusiastically, waving a hand to show they knew what to do.

"I am pleased that all the children know but I must caution you. It is not to be misused. You must believe you are mortal danger." That caution dropped most hands. "Tell me all together what the signal for immediate help is."

"Press any button three times," they chorused.

Maggie reviewed what that meant. "Any floor, the door closer button, the door opener button. Press…"

"Any single button, three times," the children shouted and clapped as they shouted. "one, two, three."

"And remember it is a secret." The room went quiet. "Now, it must be bedtime. Sleep well."

As parents and children exited, Maggie sat down with a fresh coffee with Jacob, "Thanks for being the extra eyes that recognized Felice. She'd never have gotten through the police lines if you hadn't seen her waving. She was so embarrassed about leaving the case. It was having the pile of files slide out of her arms that set that up. By the time she's pulled everything back and picked it up, all she could think of was getting out of the way of the avalanche of others who were tripping over her."

"I am sort of surprised about your comments and the emergency procedure in the elevator. Do you really have that much of a security problem?"

"The short answer is yes. And because we have so many families or women all from violent and vindictive pasts, our collective risk is that much more. Because we as a group shelter each other, we are all on the firing line for each other's attackers should they return."

"But nobody can get past the elevator, can they?"

"There is the fire escape. Those with evil intent could force the outside door but they can't get off the stairs into any floor without explosives. And they'd have to get past a couple counter measures."

"Such as?"

"The ones I can tell you about are the gates that come down on the stairs above the business levels to keep invaders out of the housing and education space.

They drop into place at any unauthorized entry into the stairwell. Anyone who got that far would need serious machinery and they'd have to contend with some busy friends."

Jacob raised his eyebrows instead of speaking.

"We have bee colonies as part of our food production. Should anyone break into the stairwell, the same alert that slams those gates also blows an air force of bees mixed with a pheromone that makes the bees really angry, into the lower stairwell. It was the idea of one of our residents who said her former companion was allergic to bees. We've never used it but it brings a great deal of comfort to all who know they have such protection."

"You said there were other measures also," Jacob urged.

"I also told you I couldn't tell you what they were."

"Got it," he said. "Time for me to go."

On his way home, Jacob fell to reflecting on the Emergency Drill. What was it like to live so precariously that you needed to rehearse your escape plan? Well he did work in a very tall building - taller than any ladder on a fire truck. He'd heard of people being caught on the roof elsewhere, by fire. He had to admit he was looking forward to the next drop down the tube. Stairs would never have worked that well.

He also began to wonder if what he was teaching was all that helpful. If you taught people to question, were they doomed to an existence as an outsider? Well his own experience taught him how blind obedience, while quite social, sure made you a victim of group myopia. On balance, he preferred the rush it gave him to examine all his old tenets and come to conclusions that gave new meaning to his life even if it meant he had to keep them to himself.

8

"Philosophical topics get tangled up easily in religious ones," Jacob began. "I suspect that was because religious people had time to contemplate because someone else was feeding and housing them so they could perform the temple duties that they were required to perform to placate whatever deities they served. Another group who had time to sit about and think were the wealthy. They survived on the toil of slaves whose efforts enriched, fed and housed those who owned them. If they weren't inspired to lofty or deep thought themselves, they could hire, or buy thinkers or scribes who could convey the thoughts of others. I think you get the idea that what was written down and what survives today, was the musings of a very select group."

"But every time I pick up a text about ancient thought, I'm reminded of those who grew the wheat and tended the vines and orchards that put the food on the thinker's tables. The process of growing food is monotonously repetitive and, I believe, can inspire deep insight, even revelation. But those thoughts never made it from that peasant thinker into today's world. Nobody wrote them down."

"It should offer us a wonderful feeling of exhilaration and freedom to realized that we might share thoughts with unknown ancient people, if we will only work to think about the awesome space about us. But those people from whenever toiled at hard labour and out of those efforts came their insights. It would be egotistical to imagine we could become similarly enlightened without effort. Yes, we might be inspired randomly by the most amazing insight. But then again, it might only be cerebral noise. So that is why we will look at what we can that remains from earlier thinkers and spend time talking about how we know that those people really said what we read. My instructions were to stay away from religion. That is not a problem given the other sources I've mentioned. So, I'm going to pick one to start with and his name was Σωκράτης." Jacob was showing off his limited skill in Greek as he wrote.

"He was so famous, as a teacher, that his name is given to a standard technique for teaching. It is a way of asking and answering questions that is intended to stimulate critical thinking. That's what we're here for: to ask and answer questions and think critically."

"Let me tell you about this person." Jason stepped to his side boards. He wrote 'NOW' at the top and then walked down the board drawing a continuous line all the way to the back of the room. "This is called a timeline and it is to tell you something special about the man. Tell me when you were born ... Daryl."

Daryl proudly declared the date and Jacob put a bar across the timeline a few millimeters from the start and his name. Many younger children called out their dates of birth and he piled up bars on top of Daryl's and added their names.

"My birth date is about here," Jacob said and added a separate bar two finger-widths from the class line. Before anyone could ask how old he was, he was walking to the back of the room saying, "and our feature teacher was born way back here in …" he wrote the date as he spoke, "489 BCE, in the country of Greece, a city called Athens."

"My Mom comes from Athens," said Markos.

"So, you might be related?" added Jacob. He wanted to move on but was diverted by the next question.

"What does BCE mean?"

Jacob let out a big sigh, "It means 'Before the Common Era' and it isn't the point of our lesson so if I answer your question, it is the last one today till I've said what I want to say." There were general *ok's* from around the room.

"If you come up to the date when the Common Era starts, it would be about here." He put mark across the timeline. If this is year '1CE', then all our dates are measured from it till now." He put bars at the millennia points. "So, if that is the first year of the Common Era, then time before that has to be numbered backwards. The year before the first year of the Common Era would have been 1 BCE. He added another close mark to the timeline. And we can see that the man of our lesson was born in," he walked back to that point, "was born in 470 or 469 but he died in 399 BCE." Jacob added a new mark, "He was seventy years old by then." There was puzzled silence.

Finally, Mary broke it, "The year after he was born, when he had his first birthday, was the year 468 BCE.

"Right," encouraged Jacob and put a tiny dot at the first birthday point. "So, when he went to school it was here, and graduated, here, and so on …" He added dots progressing through gradually smaller numbers to the date of his death. Some children got it.

"It's like you are on a countdown clock till you die," a senior added to help. More nods of understanding.

"So why didn't the dating system start with …"

Jacob's hand shot up, "My turn."

The questioner pulled his hand down.

Jacob held up his hand to reinforce the earlier deal and looked at every student. Their own hands went down; conversation stopped, "Here's my point and it is for you to think about till next day and forever."

"Our man was not an attractive child and he kept all his deformities as an adult. His nose was flat, his eyes bulged out and his lips were thick. His Dad trained him to be stonemason. He was a loyal and courageous foot soldier, rescuing a wounded friend on the battlefield."

"He was about the same height as everyone else but he adopted annoying habits like not taking a bath. He irritated people throughout tyrannical times with his analyses of their corrupt practices. When people did reply, he humiliated their empty, trivial responses. The teenagers really liked that and started to imitate him. That made their parents boiling mad. 'Know your place.' 'Do what I say,' was how parents reacted to their children trying out their teacher's practices at home."

"He treated women as equal to any aristocratic male. That got him in trouble with the men. He spoke to slaves like they had something of value to share and lived in poverty himself. That made wealthy people angry and confused about associating with him. Slaves and the poor will think they are as good as we are," they said.

"He refused to take money for the 'lessons' he taught. He claimed to hear voices directing him to do some things but not others. That was spooky and even more outrageous when he claimed he was pursuing divine goals. And in all that, he strode around like an aristocrat." Jacob snatched up the metre stick from the chalk trough and strode around affecting a sneering arrogance. The students chuckled and laughed.
"And in the end, he was condemned to death for standing almost alone in opposition to despots of his time."

He snapped back into character. "And twenty-five hundred years later we remember this social misfit. How is that possible?"

Into the silence, one student, with pen in hand and looking at the name on the board at the back of the room. "How do you say the man's name, Sir."

"Our English language grew from the Latin language used by the Roman Empire." He drew a line under the timeline. "They were as impressed by the man as we continue to be. They wrote his name like this - Sōkrátēs. We call him …" and he dramatically wrote it in capitals as he said it, "SOCRATES!

He had to review how to say it. It was not about wooden boxes. "Three syllables," he said.

Most sensed the lesson was over and started to make their notes from the board. In that shuffle, Jacob heard a stage-whispered exchange, "Yeah, they put up pages on their calendars each month instead of tearing them off?" Some children snickered. Others put their heads down to hide their smiles.

Jacob just sighed.

9

Jacob was talking to his ecclesiastical colleague, one of the few who still talked to him, on the phone. It was his house that Jacob was 'sitting' while his friend finished a post-graduate degree in UK. Each had asked the other about the past months.

Jacob was pleased to describe finding a life outside the confines in which he had served for so long. He went on to describe his duties and pupils. "It's like a Sunday school class for heretics of all ages," he concluded. "In fact, the mentioning of any deity is frowned upon. It is a really United Nations of religious backgrounds. So, we stick to Critical thinking skills applied to any philosophical topic." When he reported he was actually making a salary that made him feel wealthy, it brought a whistle from his companion.

"God works in mysterious ways," his listener said.

"We both know that random events might better explain things and save the necessity of dealing with the

Divine control that booted him from his former community and what that must say about them. If God is saving me by jerking me out of that community, it is news I don't think they'd like to hear," Jacob retorted. "Better explain it Satanically. It will get more acceptance."

"Well my time here has blossomed into a full-time position as well and my wife was offered an associate placement in the same congregation. We won't be coming back any time soon and need our equity in the house to buy something over here. That is the sad news. You'll have to move out by summer so I can sell it."

Jacob thought about that for a moment.

"What are you going to ask for the place?" he asked.

"No idea. I'll have to get an agent to sell it for me and do all the legal stuff. Really don't know what else to do. But I'd like to be able to put a down payment on a place at my new charge by August at the latest."

"Could I make an offer on it? There are legal types in the building I work in and I could get an appraisal through them. If I could put together some financing here, it would serve both our needs."

"Sounds almost too good to be true," came the surprised voice from the telephone.

"Don't tell me about a deity who deals in realty. Let me get back to you within the week … say …," Jacob named a date.

*

"What's that?" asked Brian pointing to the cut glass ash tray into which Jacob had been collecting the shavings from sharpening his pencil.

He handed Jacob his assignment as he spoke. Jacob accepted the work and set it aside as he continued to shave away thin slices of wood with the keen edge of his pocketknife. With each sliver removed, he rotated the pencil slightly ready to make the next cut. It was hypnotic to watch the pieces rise smoothly from the blade.

"There used to be a social habit called smoking." he explained. "It is dreadfully bad for your health but people did it anyway and were addicted to it. The problem was what did one do with the lighted cigarette when you wanted that hand to do something else with. Yes, you could hold it between your lips but many people set it on the edge of a table and forgot it and it burned the table or whatever. You can imagine how your Mom would react to that." Jacob didn't even look up for a response.

"Other times the cigarette fell off the table into something that burned. I can't tell you the number of fires those things started. So, someone invented the ash tray to collect the ashes and the burning ones and to try to give the habit further value, made the receptacles attractive - like this one. This is my reminder of how some people try to turn a vice into something attractive, even virtuous. And it holds these pencil slivers."

"No, I meant the thing you are cutting."

"This pencil?"

"I haven't seen one," he said.

"It is for writing with. But the lead wears down and gets dull so your lines get thicker and it is harder to read. Every so often you have to renew the point so that is what I was doing. I carry this pocketknife to do that."

"Why don't you use a pen?"

"I make a lot of mistakes. With a pencil I can rub them out with the eraser on the other end." Jacob showed the worn pink blip on the other end. "I also like to doodle and with a pencil, I can shade my drawings. Pens don't do that as well - for me." Brian's eyes flicked to the decorated margin of the page in front of Jacob.

"I also like a pencil because it makes light marks, and thick marks and thin marks." He turned the page so that Brian could see as he pointed them out. Pens are ok for light and dark but not for thick and thin so much." He'd gone back to scraping the bevels on his cutting smooth, to make a perfectly shaped shaft to a needle point. The child watched with interest.

Jacob held the finished point up for inspection, turned it and blew away the dust of a final scrape.

"Can I try it?"

Jacob pointed to an empty corner on his doodle page, "Press gently, at first. The point will break easily."

Brian slowly and carefully wrote his name then held up the page with pride, for inspection.

"Nicely done," Jacob complimented.

"Would you like it?" Jacob asked.

"Yes please, but I don't know how to sharpen it."

"Well I can show you as part of our philosophy studies," joked Jacob. "Or you can use this mechanical sharpener I keep here." He slid open a desk drawer and pulled out a blocky gadget with a hand crank on the side and a clamping lever that, when pushed down, held the instrument onto the edge of his desk. From the same drawer came a brand-new pencil. Jacob secured the sharpener, pushed the proper end into the hole and spun the handle three times. When he pulled it out a smooth sharp point graced the end of the new pencil.

"It chews up pencils pretty fast. That's another reason I like to sharpen my own. I think it also gives me a change in my pace of doing things that is worth continuing. It sort of says that one should always be ready for things and to be so, takes time, like sharpening a pencil perfectly does. There is always the hurry-up option," he nodded at the mechanical one, "but it is a small pleasure to do that." He nodded again at the one he had given Brian. "I'm big on enjoying the small pleasures that life offers."

The chime announcing the hour sounded through the public address system. Students stood as they finished and laid their work on Jacob's desk. Brian quickly gathered a group around him to admire his new tool as he left for another class.

10

"How do you know …," the students groaned quietly and collectively. Jacob realized he had probably used that opening line too often so he stopped. Instead he spread out on his display material in three small stacks on the tables down the middle of the room.

"This pile has cartoon characters you've probably seen." He set down the first pile of pages stapled in pairs. "This next pile is sayings from people. And these are photocopies of paper money currently in circulation. Take from whatever interests you and form yourselves in groups. Each group must have at least one person with paper from each pile."

The scramble for the comics and money left all but two of the pages of sayings still on the table. Then the hassle about forming the required groups started. "Well why don't you take the sayings," said one to the rest of his group. "I don't want to be in this group."

Jacob let it go on until eventually, it gridlocked. He held up a hand for attention. "The point of this part of the lesson is to make clear how little people like to discuss what people said compared with other alternatives - and to illustrate how few in a group take the trouble to do it. I need you to remember these moments when we come to wrap up our lesson."

"Now I want you to reorganize into new groups. Everyone with the same material gets into a group. The group can be big or small but everyone in it has the same material." He pointed to the corners of the room where each group should gather.

Everyone shuffled to their places. "The task now is to decide about the material you have at hand. Each collection contains material that is real and counterfeit. The cartoonist who made some of these pictures," he held up a package, "was hugely popular, syndicated around the world, in many languages. He was so popular, he was copied. You have to spot the copies and tell me how you know it is a fake."

A rustle of pages and conversation surged up. "Wait, please. Let me finish. Those with the pictures of money have pictures from the government to help people discover fake from genuine bills. And of course, my readers over here must read the sayings and decide if they came from one person or many. Each group has the work of at least two people. Questions?"

The room filled with chatter and waved paper as the children fell to their tasks - except the readers. They slouched in their seats and snorted at the wry one-liners.

"Read number twelve," It brought a snort and head toss from his companion. "I think eight is pretty sexist," she replied.

He had to occasionally go to the comic group to remind them that they were trying to find out how many people had made the characters even though they looked alike in each strip. The point was not to read them to each other or make up their own. The kids with the money photos needed little direction. They were already sorting and pointing to the diagnostic features they had spotted. He directed them to start filling in a portion of the board on the side wall with the qualities they had isolated. The readers grudgingly agreed to share what they had discovered. He asked them to elaborate on the term Mary had written before she could sit down.

"Well, 'STYLE' or 'VOICE' might need some descriptors to the others who thought you were reading, not listening, to those statements."

"Ok," she said with a huff. "Look at how short it is. If it goes to three sentences, this person likely didn't make it up," she said pointing to selections which were single sentences.

"But isn't brevity the soul of wit," her companion almost quoted. "It is the style of any one-liner to be short and pithy. What makes them traceable to one person is the sound of it, the 'voice of the time.' So, I say we have three authors here. From previous experience and extensive reading, I'd say they were Oscar Wilde, Bernard Shaw, and maybe Noel Coward."

Jacob looked at him incredibly shocked. He was perfectly correct.

"Oh, - a computer search," said the student as he waved a cell phone. "I just plugged the words in for a few and started to get repeated names so I guessed."

Trying to recover his aplomb, Jacob said, "Outside authority." He wrote it on the board, "would be your ultimate way of deciding original from copy? Have you any idea how many people contributed to the data you just presented from a database the phone connects to?" He waved at the smart phone. "Was it only one, like you, needing to get a job done fast, or was it many learned scholars?"

"I presume the scholarly host."

"The key word is 'presume'. Will you bring that up later? In the meantime, could you use your search engine to find out the origin of those identifications you collected. That is going to be really important to our discussion later."

Jacob turned to the paper money group, with a sigh. *Kids are so smart these days,* he thought. "Good progress group," he commended. "Could you put the criteria you deduced up on the board."

When he got to the Comic group, he asked the fastest writer to put up the list the kids had created. While the writers at the board finished, he gathered up the illustrative material. Children opened their notebooks.

He took a few minutes to tap at his tablet as the alarm on his phone silently flashed that he had to finish quickly.

"So, you have each have made a list of the qualities of authority in your various contributions today. You have accurately spotted fact from fiction most of the time. That was the point of today's lesson. Write down your points and then these." He wrote on his board at the front, Qualifications of expert(s), Number of similar opinions from different disciplines, Social pressures to follow, Leave room for doubt. As he finished writing, he renewed what he was saying. "It is the motto of one of the most prestigious think-tanks in the world, the Royal Society in England, that I offer. In yellow chalk he wrote:
Nullius in verba

"What does that mean?" asked Brian.

"It is Latin. You remember … From the Roman Empire? … a language said to be dead now because nobody speaks it anymore, so it doesn't change its meaning with time." He pointed to the words as he translated, 'Take nobody's word for it.'

All but one immediately started to write. Ez, the reader, who had shocked him with the on-line search of the quotes, was slouched back in his chair with his hand up and a smile on his face.

"How do you know those words mean what you say they do?"

Every eye came up at the challenging tone in the student's voice.

Jacob was ready. He picked up first his Latin dictionary. He thumped it down and on it he plopped a Latin textbook with a bookmark sticking out prominently, and then he handed across his tablet showing the webpage of the Royal Society with the motto and its translation graphically and regally illustrated. Jacob pointed to his points on the board.

Ez looked up and gave a small laugh. He handed back the tablet then picked up his own pen. As he left the classroom, he stopped beside Jacob's pile of materials. "Does the bookmark actually translate that motto?"

"Good point," said Jacob. "No that was just for show and to make it look like I knew. It is a pedagogical trick that was an illusion implying that a whole social organization was behind my statement. Good question." He pointed to his third point on the board. "But if you look here," he opened the dictionary, to the the first word in the motto, … "

Ez showed no interest in leaving for his next class. He had to look up each other word and make up alternate expressions for the motto and quibble about wording.

When he finally finished, Jacob reached into his wallet and pulled out a small sheet of stickers. From it he peeled one and asked for Ez's hand. The student put if forward curiously. When he pulled it back, he looked at the back of his hand.

"I never got one of those, before," he said with a smile.

"You earned it today. Well done! Gold star!"

11

In the end, Tina could not keep Brian's father from seeing him. He had no interest in his daughters. They were girls. Boys were what he wanted. The birth of daughters had been only one of the many reasons Tina and the children had to flee for their lives.

The court order and the slick lawyer who had accompanied it prevailed despite the efforts of Maggie and the community's lawyer. Tina's pleading and lack of proof of her claims the father's sociopathic behaviour did no good. The proceedings had ended with strict timelines and conditions under which the parent could collect and spend the day with his son. Bang went the gavel! Next case!

So, Brian's Dad pulled up in his limousine waved the court order in Barak's face and demanded his son be brought down to him as required. Father was not permitted to use the elevator.

On returning from outings, Brian regularly sported expensive gifts. Sport shoes, electronics, and candy had been noticed by Barak on previous occasions. So, it was not surprising to him when Brian returned on this day in late fall wearing a very pricey winter coat zipped right up to the neck. What was peculiar was the way he walked so slowly across the lobby to the elevator. The limo was already gone - dropped the kid like a hot brick. No lobby hugs. No endearing wishes.

Barak picked up his phone and tapped the speed dial number.

"Community Police," answered the firm voice from the office in the basement level.

"Barak here. Brian just came back and something is wrong. He didn't greet me as he usually does and he walks funny." No more description was needed about who was calling or about whom. They knew.

Barak was watching as the elevator Brian had summoned arrived loaded with clients from the offices and Jacob, heading home. He watched as Brian stepped into the elevator and the doors closed.

"Well, can't do much about funny walks or being silent," came the voice. "Neither is a crime."

Barak was replying to Jacob's wave of recognitions as he approached the desk.

And then the klaxon sound of the emergency bell in the Police Office blasted through the phone.

"Elevator," the voice snapped to her compatriot in the office and then to Barak "Got to g…" Empty air!

Jacob only saw the horrified expression replace the welcoming smile just as he got to the desk.

"Brian's in trouble," Barak said. "Basement." He was already hitting another speed-dial number.

Jacob spun on his heel and dashed for the elevator where he had last seen the child.

"Stairs," shouted Barak.

Jacob took them two-at-a-time and burst out into the parking area to see both police in firing position weapons levelled at the shaking child standing in the open elevator door.

"Brian. What's wrong?" asked the first officer already putting his pistol away.

"Can't hear you son. Speak up," said the second still ready to fire.

"I think I'm wearing a bomb," Brian said weakly.

The first officer took several steps backward. The other stepped sideways between two parked cars. "Why do you think you are wearing a bomb?"

"I overheard my Dad's friend talking in the other room. He said "When he unzips it, it will go Bsssh. And the coat is kind of heavy for feather filling."

"Step forward out of the elevator. Stop there," ordered the officer after Brian had taken five steps. That is when the officer noticed Jacob for the first time. The elevator door slid closed.

"Sir, step away from the child."

Jacob ignored the order. "He's my student," he shouted back and turned to Brian.

"Tell me Brian." He looked at the child right in the eye.

"There are square blocks in the pockets. I can feel their shape but the pockets are sewn closed. I overheard my Dad's friend say that if I didn't take it off, there was a timer. They argued about how long to set it for thinking I couldn't hear through the bathroom door. The driver and my Dad said that traffic was usually bad so to set it for more time. I think he said it was thirty minutes and it started when he zipped it up on me as we got into of the car.

"Do you think there might be ten minutes left?"

"I don't know."

The police officer continued to shout orders to move away.

"Let me feel the coat, Brian." Sure enough there were four blocks, and wires that he could feel through the fabric running up and down the front of the coat. There was another smaller chunk in an inside breast pocket. There were no wires in the back or collar of the coat that he could feel.

"Brian, turn around. I'm going to try to take this coat off you without using the zipper. I 'm going to cut it up the back."

His pocketknife was in his hand and he had the blade open as the child turned. Both police had heard Brian and stopped their own shouting. Jacob felt anew for anything in the bottom hem and then sliced through the coat. His fingers ran ahead of the razor-sharp blade feeling for wires as he worked up the center back to the neckline. A flutter of feathers fell around them in a halo on the floor. He spread the coat wide.

"Can you pull your arms out slowly?"

"Am I going to die?" Brian asked as he easily slid his arms out of the roomy coat.

Jacob's voice caught. "We've both got lessons tomorrow so I don't think so. What a way to try to get out of homework," he sighed.

"Now, tuck your chin and we'll lift this over your head. Can you get your chin inside the zipper without moving it?"

The child wiggled his neck and shoulder shrugged as the collar slid up his neck and past his ears. Feathers were flying all over the place. As the coat came free, red digits glowed out from the inside pocket and they were counting down.

"Into the stairs and run!" Jacob directed.

"Maybe a minute," shouted Jacob and lobbed the garment toward the cement cylinder collecting garbage beside the elevator. He turned to follow Brian into the stairwell but the door was locked.

"Run!" Jacob shouted as he spun the child around and they raced down the aisle lined with parked cars.

"Between the cars," ordered Jacob and Brian dodged sideways. They both ducked down, panting, waiting for the explosion. It didn't come.

"OK," came the call from back by the elevator.

In a swirl of feathers, the second officer was leaning against the wall, tatters in his hand.

He straightened as Jacob and Brian came back. "Seen that sort in training," he said. "I got the battery out in time." He tapped a double AA on the ground with his boot. He took a big breath.

"How you feeling, lad?"

Brian was white as a sheet. He nodded.

"Come and sit down by me," gestured the policeman.

Brian shook his head and moved away to a post opposite the guard and out of the drift of feathers. Jacob went with him. The child would not let go of his hand.

"I think I'll have to get your fingerprints, sir and take a statement as soon as we get the young lad looked after. Ambulance is one the way." To the other officer he said, "Go up and set off one of our smoke grenades on the top floor patio? I'll fill out the paper but do it fast."

A security guard burst out of the stairwell and stopped in the open door. "Phone Barak to stand down," said the policeman. "Clear the top floor patio. Officer headed that way. Problem solved." The Security guard ran back up the stairs.

The first officer was already talking into her communicator and headed towards their office at a run. Jacob and Brian sat on the cool concrete floor and he put an arm around the child's shoulders. They were shaking violently as the kid spun and hugged Jacob hard.

"You are the bravest boy I know," Jacob whispered into the child's ear. "Breathe deeply. Now again. Keep going." That's what he was saying when the paramedic arrived.

The paramedic sized things up immediately. The child was not going to let go of the adult. He beckoned Jacob over to the open doors of his vehicle.

"Brian, they want us to take a ride with them …"

"Brian grabbed hold even tighter.

"No, I'm not going to let you go. It's just they need us to ride over to the hospital so you can be checked."

"No," whimpered the child.

"I'm coming with you. You can hold onto me every minute." Jacob had struggled to his feet by sliding his back up the wall while carrying the boy. He'd walked to the back door of the ambulance when he said. "Brian, the step is too high for me to get in with you. My knees are too old. But if I put you down inside, can you pull me up so we can sit on that nice couch they have?"

Brian turned to look at the situation silently. Jacob set him gently inside the ambulance and reached around to grasp his arms and pull them from around his neck. Not letting go, he said. "Ok, you hold my left hand and pull. I'm going to grab the handle there," he nodded to the handhold, "and a foot up on this bumper …ok." He took a rather theatrical breath. "Pull!"

"Thanks," Jacob said. "You're stronger than you look. Can we sit down now?" He took a step further into the space leaving Brian closest to the door.

"Are you the child's father?" asked the paramedic.

Brian shook his head as Jacob said, "No, I'm his teacher and just happened to be going through the lobby when his parent dropped him off. His Mom works in the building. I don't know if she knows about this yet."

Brian gave the room number.

As he spoke, he could see Tina running out of the stairwell towards the ambulance.

It was a tearful embrace, one-armed for Brian. He was not letting go of Jacob's hand, so Tina sat on the gurney on the opposite side of unit. The paramedic wiggled past and started the paperwork as they rode to the hospital.

*

"I don't know what surprised me more," Jacob said, "not hearing the explosion, or hearing the office say it's ok. That guy deserves a medal." They were in Tina's apartment. Maggie and the community doctor sat across the coffee table. Tina completed the circle now that Brian was finally in bed and asleep.

"I recall throwing the coat towards the concrete garbage can but is fell across the rim. I just remember those numbers. I think the first one was a 'one' and the others were counting down. That's when Brian found the stairwell door was locked. But that cop must have stepped forward as we passed him to get that battery out. Je … ," he caught the epithet, "that took guts.

"And cutting my son out of live suicide vest, didn't?" said Tina. She burst into tears again. The doctor beside her reached to hand her tissues from the box on the coffee table.

"In the moment, it never occurred to me to do anything but what I did. It was like Brian and I were in this silent bubble and he was telling me something he'd seen in a book." I remember there was some noise outside and that it was annoying but it was just like we were in the classroom doing the diamond pattern thing again solving another abstract philosophical problem."

"Well, for what it's worth," said Maggie, "the policeman said that as soon as he saw it draped over the container with the wires and blocks so exposed, he recognized the style from his training. He did take a chance but he was right. He said he'd have dropped it into the container at the three-second mark if he hadn't disarmed it and hit the floor right beside the container. The concrete would both deflect the blast and protect him more than a car might. By the way, he asked if you'd come in and make a statement. I said you would be there tomorrow."

Jacob nodded.

"How is it that you cut the coat off?" asked the doctor. Surely you don't walk around with scissors in your pocket. And why didn't you pull it over his head?"

Jacob shrugged. "It looked cinched at his waist. I couldn't feel any wire in it but it did look like it would take some wiggling to get out of. Besides, I had this. He wiggled and pulled out his pocketknife. He opened the blade and handed it across.

The doctor eyed the keen blade. "Well that is even more antique. Is this to whittle while you wait for the bus?"

"I use it to sharpen my pencils," he said absolutely straight-faced.

The doctor shook her head and laughed gently as she handed it back, handle first.

As he closed it, Jacob pulled a fragment of feather from the hinge.

12

Jacob had found that a few of the students would rather draw pictures of the people he talked about in his lessons. He just wished they had drawn them on paper.

It was disconcerting when the first artist held up his tablet to show his work and even worse when the child, "Let me have yours, sir and I'll transfer it to you." In seconds Jacob was staring at the image on his own tablet.

"I presume there is a way to make comments and assign a mark." Jacob said trying hard not to look as incompetent as he felt.

"Sure," said the child. "Press here and you can type your comments," the child typed in his name as a demonstration, "then press that one… no the one beside it …and it appears on my screen …see?" And he tipped his tablet over to show the drawing with his name now in place below.

Staring up at Jacob from the glass screen was a clone of the kid's work. It took him a moment to get used to the feel not being of paper. It didn't bend, or rustle in his fingers. There was a missing warmth. He had to shake his head to get back to the subject at hand - the student's way of completing the assignment.

Deciding it was as valid a way of thinking critically, for their age, he'd encouraged the artistic response. Suddenly finding the reply flitting around like a phantom was ... disconcerting. *Move on, Eiger,* he thought. *Look at the work, not the fact that you've slipped a gear.*

The artwork from the various students ranged from copies of statues or paintings of Socrates to comics and caricatures. Again, Jacob was astonished at the maturity of the replies of the young artists to his questions.

"Do you think that sculptor really knew what Socrates looked like?" The student's work could have been a photograph.

"Well the statue is not like you described him, so I think the artist made it up. This is complete fiction. But the sculptor was trying to convey authority, power, and he was doing it for someone who wanted a nice decoration. So, you give the buyer what they want. By making him look like a god, and putting a famous name on it, everybody was happy."

The comic strip artist had portrayed Socrates as a sad, person with some regard to the description Jacob had given. It was the others gathered around for the suicide who were portrayed grotesquely, with absurd proportions. "Well I think this is what Socrates was trying to say about the society - how distorted their lives were by the pursuits that obsessed them."

Jacob asked them to describe their work and their insights to the whole class. When everyone settled, Jacob introduced the subject for the day by holding up paintings.

"Can you see the philosopher figure?" Children pointed to them correctly.

"And my favourites," he added after the chattering subsided.

It was the art students who swept them up when everyone else looked up at him to see what he would say. Jacob saw the move and signed for the pictures to be pinned up at the front.

"Any doubt about who our man is in the pictures?" A chorus of 'No's' sounded.

"This was the original homeless man. He was homeless before there was a name for the situation and he was so by his choice. He is famous today because of his effect on those around him in his day - which by the way was back just after Socrates." He walked to the side of the room where his timeline still waggled along the top of the board and followed it to the back of the room where he added marks at 412 and 404 BCE.

"We're not sure when he was born. During his lifetime, the man never wrote a word, but my how he could speak. And he didn't just talk the talk, he walked the walk. His name was Diogenes. "It's said with four syllables," and he pronounced them out and put a vertical line between the 'i' and the 'o'. Of course the children grabbed the other way to say the name and laughed as they traded it around.

"He was born here," he pointed, to the wall map and the town in Turkey on the bump on the south shore of the Black Sea, "in the town of Sinope."

"His father was a banker and responsible for minting the coins that everyone used. Somehow Diogenes got connected to the business of shaving off the proper amount of gold or silver that was supposed to be in each coin and replacing it with something worthless. When the fraud was discovered. Diogenes was convicted and exiled instead of executed." He had to explain exile.

"Diogenes was penniless when he moved to Athens. We don't know what he did there but he became outraged at how many people spent their whole lives making themselves wealthy at everyone else's expense. They cheated, abused, exploited; they were really mean. Diogenes said that the goal of life was to be in harmony with nature, lead a simple life. But he said you couldn't just say that. You had to do it and he did by example. That is why he is shown in the picture living in a wine barrel," he pointed to it, "or naked and begging for food."

"He quickly came to the attention of everyone. The man had a wonderful wit and this is the subject of one of the most powerful stories about his life. One day he was found walking through town in broad daylight with a lighted lantern. 'What are you doing?' he was asked. 'I'm looking for an honest man,' was his reply. We don't know if he meant honesty as 'one who did not cheat' or one who was honest enough to admit to personal failings or distraction. It is why he is regularly depicted with a lantern." He pointed the lanterns in the pictures.

"How bright does it have to be to be able to see such a person? Apparently, you can't see one in the brightest light. He suggests it is because there aren't any. And then there is my favourite, the one without the lantern. Just a ragged peasant sunning himself against a wall when a soldier stands before him. The soldier, Alexander the Great - the most powerful man in the country - a General who led his armies to conquer most of the known World at the time." He pointed to the map he'd hung earlier.

"So, there they are. The greatest power in the land standing in front of a beggar and the soldier says to the beggar, 'I can give you whatever you want. What is it you want?' Wow! What do you think he'd ask for?" He quickly held up a restraining hand. "Don't tell me yet. Let me tell you and you can then tell me if you guessed correctly."

"So, Diogenes looked up at this powerful person and said, … Jacob waved a hand to imitate the sage. 'I'd like it if you would just move over. You're standing in my sunshine.'"

"That's all he wanted. For the man to move over. Did you guess correctly?" Everyone laughed.

"Diogenes was delivering a whack at commercial life and the pursuit of possessions we all follow. We hear that comment still, from thousands of years ago and half a world away. We'll be studying the Cynic School he helped to found in our next lessons. For now, make your notes from the board."

*

Maggie summoned him to meet in her office when the news of his philosophy lessons got around. Students were taking them far too much to heart. She sat on the other side of a desk half the size of a tennis court. He was invited to sit on a hard chair.

"Your philosophy lessons have been making an impact," she began. But the way she said it made Jacob suspect there was more to come. He didn't have long to wait.

"Parents are complaining to me that their teenage children, especially, are questioning every rule that comes up. Bedtime, food they must avoid, why they need to plan to get a job. I've heard it more than once that 'the unexamined life is not worth living.'"

"That's Socrates," Jacob interjected.

"Well it's getting to be a problem."

"Odd, Socrates found the same. So did Diogenes."

"Who?"

"Two of the people we've been studying. They were immensely popular with the youth of their day for just this reason, and not so much with the parents - again for exactly the same reason."

"Well I need it to stop. I'm hearing the request for appointments with our psychologist for depression, anger management, even suicide have jumped hugely in recent weeks. Moms who come from battered pasts you can't imagine are being pushed to the edge. They already feel they are juggling all the balls they can and if they get one more challenge, they'll drop the whole bunch. Each can only stay here till they have the skills to keep themselves safe and secure when they leave. But they must leave. These challenges from their kids are interfering with the corporate mission to extend our help to many others. We'll be getting a reputation as the place to avoid if our Mothers wind up with more problems when they leave, than when they came in."

"Whoa, wait a minute. These women already have these problems when they arrive. The feeding and vocational responses are just your part of the remedy package. When the parents leave, they can leave wrapped up in their routines but it is unreasonable to imagine their kids won't be bringing home problems like the ones you mention. Only then, they'll be on their own and then those women you have so 'saved'," he drew the quotes in the air, "will drop all the balls, as you so eloquently put it. I'm not bringing up anything that isn't already in play. What my classes seem to have exposed is the narrowness of the plan to rehabilitate. And yes, you can thank me for being so successful at inspiring the youth." Jacob was almost shouting and stopped to try to calm down.

Maggie, too, found herself half standing, ready to fire back. The accusation stung. It had been the goal of her program to insulate and fortify her protégés, presuming it was enough to have high and hard walls. As Jacob had been talking, it was dawning on her that in fact it was the model she, herself, had been living and which had proved so successful for her. As long as she had enough wealth, it worked. Her career path in the hospital had been an extension of her rule-based life plan. Every action could be backed up by a protocol and procedure rooted in scientific study. What Jacob had exposed was the narrowness that such certainty brought. What he was doing was substituting flexibility and ways to adapt to unknowns and the uncertainty of the vision scared her.

She had been about to set Jacob in his place for not being a team player - for failing to uphold the regimentation that had been so successful in first, protecting, then improving the lives of so many who had been in this place before he arrived. No wonder he had been driven out of that strict religious community. She had been so sure that she too had to show him the door when he entered the office. But not now. Doubt nibbled at her conviction.

Both realized something hard had broken since the meeting started and the shards had sharp edges. Both realized too, that it might be better to stop and think about their next words. In that moment, Jacob realized that the sun which had been slanting through the window when he came in, casting Maggie's shadow on the chair where he sat, had moved on down the sky. Now he was squinting in the full sun. This was not the time for a smart-ass answer. He shuffled his chair sideways into the shadow of the wall.

"Look," he said, "I never thought I'd be a teacher - just a preacher. I told people what to believe and they trusted me and my divine vision. Now I think I was a fraud. When I was kicked out of that society, I reveled in the freedom to think and explore areas of thought that had been forbidden fruit most of my life. It is the most liberating thing that ever happened to me. I couldn't help sharing that with my pupils and it obviously struck a chord. They are hungry to do the same. But all those constraints they face only encourage rejection. That is how their parents, and maybe you, interpret their actions. I see those efforts as exploration - within a secure and safe framework. If it is putting cracks in the wall, maybe it is time for some repair work but it will involve the figurative architects, tradesmen, and City Council By-law officers." He stopped for a moment.

Maggie was prepared to let him talk - hang himself if he chose to. That would only make her job easier. And also, if he was talking, she didn't have to. That too, gave her more time to consider.

"It might be helpful to have those parents with issues and the students themselves, trade positions in some sort of refereed forum," Jacob suggested. "It could be by video if you thought it was a good way to start just because it gives everyone a chance to practice the dialogue without looking down the gun barrel glares of the other. When everybody has had a chance to see each other's terrain, and some rules of engagement have been agreed upon, then they could get together to work out something mutually agreeable." He stopped hoping he had offered something they could both work towards.

Maggie swiveled around and looked out the window for quite a while. Jacob just looked into his lap and waited.

"Alright," she said eventually as she swung to face him. I'll get the parents to make a list. I don't think they'd like to go on camera but I'll ask. You do the same with you students. Let's trade those lists, say ...", she looked at a calendar on her smart phone and named a date and time three days away. She was tapping it in before he agreed.

13

There was no stack of papers on the desk, no map, or pictures on the wall when the students came in - just Jacob sitting behind his desk with his head down. The kids shuffled into the seats and the chatter died when Jacob didn't say anything, not even his usual greeting.

"I was not always a teacher. I grew up in a very restricted and conformist environment. I need to tell you this because it is the basis on which today's lesson rests." He continued with his autobiography stressing particularly the restrictions of it.

"And then the community did what they did to Socrates… well not quite. They didn't make me drink poison. But they did drive me into exile from their midst." He went on to describe his isolation, his depression, and the beginnings of his resurrection when he was hired to come and teach philosophy - no religion. And finally, he got to the thrill it gave him to share this wonderful world of thought and experiment.

"Well, the consequences of taking you into that space have suddenly been made clear. Some of you really believe me. You do think that everything should be questioned. I'm flattered, even overwhelmed. But I should have laid a better foundation for the edifice I was building. Some parents are frantic, just as parents were in the days of Socrates and Diogenes, that their children are being led to the Dark Side. Suddenly, all the pain they have suffered, for longer than you've been alive, is returning. The hopes they live for with every job, they see teetering on a knife edge. So we need to go back and realize where they are coming from, and where you think you'd like to go, and assure each other that neither is blowing up the bridges that join you."

"Do you recall our first meeting when Brian brought up his broccoli problem?" It brought smiles all around. Nobody brought up his brush with death. "See much broccoli in the cafeteria lately?" More laughs. "So, this works. Let's begin by getting those of you who have been facing an exploding parent lately, stating what the problem was. If you don't want to talk about your parent, tell me about someone else you heard about who had a similar problem. Tell me what their problem was."

Jacob got a laundry list.

*

Jacob also had to appear at an adults-only meeting of the parents. He started with the rules, "Only speak through the chair, use the word 'I' to describe feelings, and avoid the word 'you'." He offered his own story as an example. What he got in return from the others was the effects of personal abuse, war, and pestilence on an international scale.

As he took notes, he could not help but be amazed at humanity's talent for terror and violence. *Is this what it is to be human?* he wondered but quickly rejected the thought. *Look at the refuge here. Look at the parents fighting to keep it that way - a place of safety and security, of kindness and consideration. They see critical analysis as the process by which the rules that keep this place going are eroded.*

Walking home, it also came to him that the society in which the Cynics lived was not the same as the situation in Lindsay Tower. He began to think of other female societies and the cloisters or female sanctuaries of medieval Europe came to mind. He began to feel the Lindsay Tower community was more like those communities that women created centuries earlier as options to the cloisters that were the alternative. Both had rules designed to keep them going as economic necessities that served the protection priority. It hadn't meant that creativity or experimental thinking was off limits. It was just knowing where the line was. That would have to be his next lesson series - Communities of Values. He liked the sound of the title. And he could do communities that valued violence, ignorance, *I wonder if there were any dedicated to harmony with nature?* He pondered. *Of course! - First Nations.*

The syllabus spread out like a carpet till Christmas.

*

"He really doesn't understand the threat we feel, does he?" Libby was talking to another Mom whose teenager had developed such a snide attitude and disdain of rules within the family and the community at large. "He was saying that he knows where they are selling drugs on the way to the Mall."

"Did you tell him that if he ever thought of using drugs, or worse, bringing them into the building to tempt others, you'd be history so fast you wouldn't have time to pack?"

"Yes, and that his Dad overdosed and died of the stuff - spent every cent I earned on his stinking habit. Maybe he needs a chance to see what living in a box on the street is like. It is only because I got in here that he isn't living in someone else's house as a foster kid." Libby was twisting her hands in anxiety. It sounded so much like her Ezra.

*

"Ez," Jacob called as the class was walking out after Monday's class. "Got a moment?" Ezra stopped at Jacob's desk.

"I gave that gold star out for exceptional thoughtful effort." Jacob had seen the star on the inside cover of Ez's notebook, close to the binding where it didn't show easily and covered by a piece of sticky tape during a book shuffle several days ago. "I'd like to challenge you to earn another - that is if you want the bragging rights to another. Maybe getting one was enough for a lifetime."

Ez tossed his head with a chuckle. He knew when he was being jerked around.

"I'd like you to try to invent a society of people like Diogenes that can sustain itself for two generations - on paper of course. You know a lot about him and the other Cynics. I'm just wondering why they didn't form a commune or something and figure it's my old brain that won't work fast enough. Could you give that a try?"

Ezra shrugged, "Ok, how long to do it?"

"Let's see what you got in a week. Comes with a milkshake at the Mall if you're done before the weekend - or do you like Sundaes or Banana splits?"

"If it comes with a spoon, that's good. If you're talking about the place, I think you are, they have something called a David Harum. Those are to die for."

"Well if you need to share your star with a friend to put a response together, feel free to invite them."

On Friday, Ez asked if he and some friends could present their study as a sort of Greek play.

"I am Reader 1, Diogenes 1," declared the first actor. He was a short, fireplug of a kid who teetered sideways back and forth as he came to the center of the room. He was holding a lamp on a pole like a lance. "Because I cannot agree on a set of conventions by which to present this play, there can be no play. He made a rude noise and teetered across to the other side of the room, where he immediately turned around, paused, and then with small steps and a purring sound, moved back to center stage.

"I am Reader 2 Diogenes 2 or R2D2, and we can only proceed by ignoring Diogenes call for no conventions which presents us with a paradox. By the act of preparing this play, we should not be able to talk about the person we are supposed to represent." He began to twirl about making whistling and popping sounds that took him offstage where he banged into a corner and stopped.

The students laughed at his caricature.

Immediately from the other side of the room, Mary stepped forward swathed in a bedsheet somewhat like a Greek gown. "I am Cordelia and this is the first parodos or act, so I am C, 1P. My robotic friend has delivered a paralyzed prologue because of the lack of operating instructions. The goal of we Cynics is calmness, love of all, and indifference to the personal changes of life. We just drift along talking about how we want to commune with nature. We wish to own nothing, but we would be glad if you, who have things, would share your dinner with us. We don't want to work, only point out how the work you do daily corrupts you and makes you subject to negative emotions and vicious behaviour towards everyone - including us."

Her monologue was interrupted by four others in the corner singing. While they sang, Mary moved off Stage Right. "... For the rest of your days... It's our problem free ... Philosophy..."

Everyone clapped and as the applause died, Mary was back, but shuffling a bit to her place at center stage.

"I am Cordelia and this is the second parados so my part is C, 2P. Diogenes said that physical training was as necessary as mental training in the practice of the virtuous life. But those attending Cynic University could never play anything like an organized game because they couldn't agree on the rules. And they couldn't organize a university either."

"So, they really were in terrible physical shape - starved, ill, and dirty. The only reason they got better, was that others cared for them. In later times, like ours, we'd say such people might be deranged, needing mental attention. They might even be locked up as public nuisances. Back then, and maybe now, such people might have served some sort of comic role or provided gossip for those with little else to talk about. Others would say they were savants. How else do your quotes last thousands of years?

As she ended the door at the rear of the classroom opened and three more students in robes entered to a guitar syncopation plucked by the Ez in the lead. The last held the door for the final group member who had his small keyboard mounted on hooks in his belt and a strap around his neck. They immediately started to sing as they danced to the middle of the room now vacated by Mary. They hit the chorus and immediately most of the children joined in.

"… Give me the open mind that I had before
I'm living with it
(Oh-oh-oh-ooh)
I'm living with it
(Oh-oh-oh-ooh)
Oh, I'm a cynic

By the time the group got to the closing verse, everyone was up waving arms over their heads in time to the music. It was not a tune Jacob could recall. "It's from Noah Kahan," the student beside him said. "You know," and she jumped up to join the rest.

"(Oh-oh-oh-ooh) …
I don't know why I see no light in anything (oh-oh-ooh)
Leave it to life to turn my strengths back into weaknesses
But I'm living with 'em
So, give me the open mind …"

The quartet danced out the front door of the room back into the hallway as their chorus ended. Everyone was applauding. When the door closed. Mary was now shuffling quickly, despite her robe, to her former place. "I am…"

The children snatched the words from her mouth "C, 3P!"

"Oh," she said instantly, "I wondered if you'd get it." Everyone laughed. "Cynics concentrated on ethics and were quick to point out failings in systems or behaviour around them. They modelled a life of poverty supposedly because it freed them to love others and seek to be self-sufficient. Nothing of those efforts is recorded. So, cynics likely had an unreported side. Though they criticized the pursuit of wealth, they could only survive in a society that blessed that pursuit."

"Cynics never created their own towns. The best they could be was a hermit. They claimed to be citizens of the world at a time when identity was rooted in where you came from. It was the default option if nobody wanted you anymore - you could always claim membership in the whole world because everywhere was spoiled by riches."

"So, cynics could only stand out in a group of conformists. Embarrassing questions were only useful to keep conformity from falling off a cliff of its own creation. Robots don't ask questions; it's why they can't be humans."

She bowed with these words and immediately the front door opened with the quartet belting out their song as they skipped back into the room.

"One more time," shouted Mary and the chorus came back, ending with a slowing of the instruments and a long strumming on the guitar. Everyone was applauding as the students took bows at the front.

Jacob was stunned. It was Maggie's touch on his shoulder that startled him.

"I didn't know you were there. I just asked Ez for a few pages on a society of Cynics. I promised him a trip for ice cream treats if he was done by Friday. Looks like I'm in for a group of half a dozen." Jacob was struggling to extricate himself from seeming to make light of those parental concerns he'd faced earlier.

"I think the kids have made it plain, that they are not really out to leave and join a commune. They are just doing what they need to do to stay safe in the uncertain world out there that we shield ourselves from by seeking more certainty inside these walls."

"Do you supposed they would do that after Dinner some night?" Maggie continued.

When they did, Ezra's mom still left, fuming mad. "So, I'm a robot? Wait till he becomes a parent."

14

There were too many to fit into the corporate van so Jacob and his entourage had to walk to the Mall so he could make good on his pledge to reward them all for their work on the Cynics. It was Ez who pointed out how ironic the indulgence of the reward was considering the topic for which it was awarded. Maggie too had asked to join them. The students had no objection. Her inclusion was why the van was simply not possible.

Jacob noticed that the Ez redirected the group to go on a different route from the most direct one to the Mall. For Jacob, it was not an issue; he liked walking, and any excuse was good enough. He was curious about the reason but not enough to ask. Maggie did ask and was greeted with a vague response. "I like to go this way," Ez said.

The group fell into twos and threes, chattering away as they walked. Jacob was really glad to see Brian was part of the group. He had been a singer in the first group singing the song from the popular movie. He still wore his jacket though nobody else was wearing one, and his hands were in his pockets the whole way. Jacob was pretty sure he knew why and was happy about it.

Because they were the adults, Jacob and Maggie were sort of shepherded into walking together by the students who clustered themselves. Maggie asked about the students as they walked but it was an empty interest. She talked about how she was currently dealing with a city bylaw that was challenging the workplace safety standards of the underground greenhouse operation beneath the parking lot. It had been built to mining standard with all the required protocols but a local politician had thought he could shut it down by saying it was a greenhouse and therefore had to be on the surface. It was just another of the constant barrage of challenges that Maggie felt that MEN threw at her to shut down her sanctuary. Jacob listened in silence as they walked.

The conversation had a contrived quality that made Jacob tingle slightly. They could have just walked along in silence, talked about the weather. There was no reason he needed to know all this stuff. In fact, the detail, and the slightly phony way it was delivered, set off a small but distant bell tinkling for his attention.

Learning to listen to his intuition was something that had grown on him since his liberation from his religious confinement. Originally, he had been dismissive of the feelings to avoid some situations or attend to others. Things crystallized when he got sick last Fall.

When he thought about it with a stuffed nose and coughing like a hospital patient, he realized maybe he had subliminally reacted to the flushed face that preceded him into the elevator and which then coughed all the way up to the third business floor in their building. He'd gone on to his class but he was bedridden two days later, and off for a week more. So, he'd started to pay more attention to the quiet voice that nagged within him sometimes. He'd at least learned to stop and listen. He'd learned to look around when that bell went off, as it did now.

The kids waited inside the Mall door for them to catch up. Jacob had always liked the walk down the hallway to the ice cream place on the Food Court. The Arts of the World window display and the non-profit group who ran it were always an attraction. He'd followed Brian's gaze and gave a small start when he spotted the tiny trouble dolls in the back corner of the window display. They had been part of Jacob's armoury when he was a pastor and had to counsel parents with troubled children. Here was a new supply.

Jacob had offered a couple to the institution's doctor who was treating Brian after the trauma of last Fall. Brian found he could tell all his worries to the tiny companions, put them in their little box and then go to sleep leaving his problems in other hands. "It beat the meds, for him," the doctor had said when he thanked him for the idea and the objects around Christmas time.

The girls in the group got hung up at the fashion store in a spirited discussion of the display. Ez joined Brian and the boys to walk past but all stopped at the Art Supplies window. An artist was doing a painting demonstration and he was talking as he did, through a speaker, to his hallway audience. They watched for a while. Brian looked back and flashed Jacob a smile as he and Ez turned away from the window. Jacob knew why. In that store, he had bought Brian a small, wooden, articulated hand that artists sometimes use as a model to do portraits or action scenes.

"If you ever need a hand and I'm out of reach, you can use this," Jacob had explained. Brian carried it in his pocket all the time. It gave them both a smile whenever they saw similar ones. The sight reminded him that he wanted to get another. "I'll join you in a few minutes," he said to Maggie.

While most dawdled over their choice from the wall menu, Ez went straight to the counter at the candy and ice cream emporium. "A David Harum double and he's paying," he hooked a thumb in Jacob's direction. Eyebrows went up on the cashier till he got Jacob's nod and finger direction that circled the group.

Brian, at Ez's elbow said he'd have the same and was corrected by the older boy. "You want a single, Brian. Trust me. Doubles are huge!" It proved to be the case. Ezra needed two hands to pick up his order.

With their assortment of sundaes, banana splits, and frozen yogurt in a dish instead of cones topped with an incredible display of sprinkles, crushed candy and syrups, the rest joined the collection of tables Ezra and Brian had assembled. Jacob ordered a large slice of Creamy Coffee Ice Cream Pie. They cut the pies here in sixths not eighths or tenths. Maggie got a single-scoop cone and sat on the edge of her seat across the table from him. Jacob was on the end of the table beside the kids at theirs. Maggie perched like an outsider.

Jacob swallowed his gasp and blinked only twice when the tally came up and he inserted his Debit card in the reader to pay. *A good education rarely came cheaply,* he thought.

As dishes were polished off, Ez observed that Diogenes never knew about ice cream when he was around. "The philosophy would have died in birth if there had been. Nobody can resist that! Say professor, is there another assignment like the one on Cynics - with similar inducements?"

Jacob laughed, "I was wondering about a study on the philosophy of capitalism and to follow this pattern for the last assignment, it should be we who should offer to serve at a meal for the homeless or at the food bank."

Jacob was surprised at the enthusiastic interest. The students went back to chatting about the possibility. Jacob muttered to Maggie "I really should learn to think before I speak."

Maggie let the comment slide. "They really are different when they are outside, aren't they?" She observed almost as though she was suddenly aware she was with the group.

"What does that say about the community, if anything?" asked Jacob. "Maybe we only see them when under instruction, as though it was a rock or something."

Again, Maggie ignored the reply. She glanced at her phone but not at a screen of emails based on the glance Jacob got of it. It was the time she had wanted. "I must excuse myself - meeting back at Action Central." She rose seemingly unnoticed by the students. "Please convey my apologies for leaving," and she was striding away, not for the door by which they had entered, but in the direction of the fountain in the middle of the Mall. Jacob followed her as she ditched her unfinished cone in a litter container before she rounded the sculpture to where she excitedly met another well-dressed woman. Together they walked further around the pool and out of sight.

Jacob sighed as he considered the misdirection and the meeting as he picked up his fork to push a couple smears of ice cream and sauce into a single row that he might still pick up. He looked up. Everyone seemed finished as well. "You all did a fine job with your presentation. I've never done this before but it seems like a really good idea for outstanding work."

Everyone approved again. "Time to go." A group had gathered at the candy display to calculate how much they could buy with their pocket money. "Well, if I buy those could, I trade you some for what you buy?"

"Can you speed that up?" Jacob asked Ezra when they met in the hallway to wait for the others. "Oh, before you do, I still owe you this." He took a gold star, still on its backing, out of his wallet and handed it over.

Ez took it and smiled as he waved it about wondering what to do with it. "What would Diogenes say?"

"Oh, and this," Jacob handed Ez a small bag.

Ez hooked the bag with a free finger below his star and pulled the articulated wooden hand free with the other. Jacob took the empty bag back.

"What's this for?"

"I think your Mom is pretty angry about any challenge to a strictly regimented life. She came by that practice out of surviving experiences she wants you to avoid. Anyway, it occurred to me that once in a while you might need a hand."

Ez looked at the joints intently and flexed the fingers. "It is almost like a real one."

"Sometimes the symbol must substitute or be a reminder of reality - like Diogenes's lamp."

Ez peeled the backing from the star and pressed into the palm of the figure then folded the fingers over it. "I'll remember that," he said without a smile. He took the bag back and dropped the hand back into it. "I'll get the others."

As Ez rounded up the students and they gathered the things they'd been carrying, Jacob's glance around the Food Court caught on a large man slouched in a booth on the far side. He seemed to be eyeing the group Ezra had assembled. Well, they were chatty kids and certainly stood out in this place. Instead of heading straight across the space, Ezra led them obliquely back towards the Art Store suggesting they look at what the artist had completed.

As they left the Mall, Ez again led the group on the longer way home. He fell in beside Jacob as they hit the residential street. Jacob walked in silence for a few moments then asked, "What was that and this about?"

"There is a drug dealer's house on the other street," Ezra said after a silence. "And that guy in the Mall is connect to organized crime, I think. Definitely bad news. He's there a lot watching people. Anyone I've seen sit at his table gets up in a few minutes. Never saw him or his companion eat anything. No papers shared like it was a business meeting. Just a touch-and-go contact. Actually, sort of creepy to watch."

"How do you know about guys like that or the house?"

Ez shrugged, "Internet. Don't need to accidentally give my Mom any more ammo."

They walked on for half a block. "You know for someone who knows so much about civilizations and communities two thousand years ago, you sure don't seem to know much about the neighbourhood."

Jacob tried to deflect the dart the bold young man had thrown. "Diogenes would say things like that but probably in reverse. For someone who knows all about the neighbourhood, you know surprisingly little about life." But what Jacob thought was, *he's too accurate.* Somehow his unawareness of his community space linked back to the moment the student presented his art on his tablet. He was still stunned by what that child did with his assignment while Jacob was still in the paint and paper world. He felt so old. *And I still write with a pencil.* He wanted to wince but decided to join Ezra in a sort of laugh.

15

In his old job as the pastor of a very conservative congregation, Jacob was the recipient of lots of gossip from those seeking to protect the morals of the community and wanting credit for the effort. Some sidled comments were malicious, some was genuinely concerned; all of it was a cross to bear as far as he was concerned.

Usually the complainant had some scripture to quote to rationalize their actions and maybe those they criticized. That was part of his problem. Usually neither was correct. His personal research of how the scriptures had come to be after the errors, editorial additions, and political infighting of the day had been stripped away, left him questioning what had originally been said. It left researchers trying to tease out the voice print from an oral tradition. Jacob had become far more ... humanistic, maybe forgiving in the face of such doubts. It was one of the big rocks thrown at him at his 'recall'. He was not defending community standards.

When he'd investigated many of the *I just thought you should know* stories, circuitously and softly, he'd usually found the 'strange man' was a distant relative, the 'missing money' was a tabulation error in the church accounts. And when such results were conveyed to the self-righteous, they were no pleased to hear the adage about those who live in glass houses.

So, when he started to overhear the scuttlebutt about Maggie's new love affair, it actually brought back a smile of satisfaction that this was no longer part of his job description. The titillation in the elevator or cafeteria lineups made him smile. The overly enthusiastic whispers across a nearby table about the lady's new wardrobe made him chuckle. The outrage over the expensive new car almost brought him to outright laughter. He caught himself in time.

The rescued souls with backgrounds in poverty were hypersensitive to such changes. While they were struggling towards self-sufficiency in the jobs they had as part of the recovery-from-abuse program, old habits died hard. How often had they suffered when a spouse had shown up similarly decked-out with flimsy excuses about where the money would come from to pay for such luxuries? How often had they endured the battering that criticism brought? Jacob said to himself that it was old wounds opened - until Ezra mentioned it at one of their regular ice cream parlour escapes.

"I saw Miss Maggie's new girlfriend talking to that guy," Ez said as he flicked a glance across the Food Court to the man, Ez claimed was some sort of local criminal.

Mary chimed in, "I saw her coming out of the street where the drug house is."

They both looked at Jacob as though he was supposed to reply. "Back when you first brought those items to my attention, I had a few words with the police in the community station back at our building." Neither needed to be reminded about how Jacob knew the officers in the parking lot.

"While the police rarely tell guys like me anything, I did detect a hint of appreciation in the 'We'll look into it' reply. That was months ago when you told me, I think they're doing their 'background checks'. Maybe if they're working on that it is better to have their suspects in plain sight than have to go looking for them again. I think we can be confident that our information has been received and is being acted upon." And that was where Jacob wanted the conversation to end.

"Tell me about your co-op job, Mary," Jacob continued.

Mary started to talk about the bank she was working in as an apprentice learning to apply her computer skills to surveillance of suspicious withdrawals. Once started she was hard to stop.

"I can't break confidentiality codes but it is really interesting. My job is to collect the list of flagged accounts each day and bring them to my boss. It is pretty menial but this is a job I could work into. My boss was surprised at what I already know and if your ears were burning lately, it was because he said that not many people think as critically as I do. He was even complimentary when he said I asked the right sort of questions. Not everybody does that, he said. For instance, once he showed me how to collect the list, I deduced how to collect background to each account by making a list of the earlier charges to the card, and how to present that with each of the suspicious withdrawals. I remember the first time I did that. He was so surprised. Considering that the new purchase that was called in as suspicious, was made at a girlie fashion place, I suggested that maybe Mom might have loaned her credit card to her daughter and then called it in as a wrong charge. Well maybe the kid did steal her Mom's card. Maybe the Mom was trying to scam the system. Maybe it was an honest mistake by a frazzled parent. Anyway, the card holder did say that she had forgotten when my boss phoned her. But I got a gold star for catching it with my background check."

"Did he really give you a gold star?" asked Ez incredulously.

"No but I told him he could have and instead, I gave him one like you did sir," she said to Jacob. "I said it was for noticing and telling me I did a good job - inspiring the troops sort of thing." She giggled at the memory of that moment. "You know it is such fun to do that. People are so…"

"'Flummoxed' is a good word," Jacob offered. Mary looked confused.

Immediately Ezra was on his smart phone. "Perplexed, bewildered," he said when the definition appeared.

"It is the philosopher effect," suggested Jacob. "Employees are supposed to be subservient. By giving him the reward and pointing out why, you usurped, for the moment, his role and he wasn't sure what to do about it. But you have to be careful about who you use it on. Some bosses might think you uppity. Don't spend time working for them long. They don't like challenges to authority they might have been given rather than earned. Thus, is says in the Second Book of Jacob the Outcast," he concluded.

Ez smiled back. "I never met a teacher like you," he said. "You seem to be a fountain of such stuff and you slip it in while nobody's looking."

"Well, it did not serve me well in my earlier life. There I had to keep my thoughts to myself, another valuable lesson. They can only harpoon you while you're spouting,' said the fisherman."

"See there's another one. What a nice way to say shut up. You should be a stand-up comedian."

"Teacher by another name. Time to go."

*

The school in Lindsay Tower, ran a trimester system. Part of the program for each child was a Co-op program. For the summer, Ezra was working in the power plant getting at least an appreciation of the way it ran and the computer programs needed to keep things balanced. He liked the trouble-shooting simulations. He was allowed to continue even though his mother had now moved out of the residence and was living independently.

For her, the program had done its job. She and Ez had barely escaped an abusive relationship with their lives. Within the Lindsay program, she had regained her health and confidence and had upgraded skills that now made her well employed and financially independent. She had to graduate to open a space for another like her to be rescued. So, there was a little departure ceremony for the graduates of the program and away they went. They all looked forward to the reunion in the Fall where they would return and share their experiences with those still in training.

Ezra's duties kept him busy. Jacob got the summer off and devoted it to his own studies of philosophy. He read a lot down by the river, commandeering a shady picnic table so much that the locals thought he might have bought it. He even brought his own patio umbrella against rainy days, leaving the cement block into which it fit, behind the nearby garbage can chained to the tree, when he went home at night.
It was not uncommon for the weather unwary to seek refuge from a flash shower under his shelter. Invariably he was asked what he was doing and he did not

disappoint his questioners. When he went on a bit long, most decided that the shower must be just about over and scurried off. But it didn't take that to convince Jacob he could never be a philosopher. He was just too pragmatic for the job as a long-term career.

He loved finding out about each new thinker whose work he studied. He loved developing the historical arc through which ideas passed. But when it came right down to it - So what! Would any of those academic pursuits of a lifetime change the price of groceries at the store? His critical thinking skills were razor sharp. He could argue both sides of any argument. And when he was done, was the place he now inhabited really different from the pulpit he had previously occupied?

But Social Work? He wondered if he had enough empathy to do that job. Maybe he'd become too much like the cynics of old that he studied. That the idea of such a service occurred to him at all was likely because of one of his regular visitors.

"Call me TD ... like the bank," The bewhiskered vagrant had said as he brushed off his stained sleeves and struck his executive pose. "Not DT. I turned my life around a long time ago. No alcohol for me now." And then he broke into song, "I'm DT-free ... It's TD's problem free ...Philosophy ... He warbled away in search of a musical key and cackle at the incredulous looks he got from passers-by. They quickly had turned and hustled away.

"There, that leaves another cup of coffee for me," he said that one particular day.

TD had been an earlier and frequent visitor at Jacob's table. Jacob had spotted the facade right off the bat. "It's ok, they're gone now," he said at their first meeting. "Have a cup." He'd gestured to the take-out carafe. "Because you're here early, it comes with a 'day-old' if I don't tell you where I got them from."

Jacob had boosted a bag out of his backpack and tore it down the side. "Sorry, no serviettes."

TD tore a crescent out of the bag and used it between his fingers to pinch a sticky donut from the display. Jacob noted the strong hands with clean fingernails and pink palms. "No need," TD mumbled around his first bite.

Jacob found a soulmate in TD. Each listened with interest to the other's stories and laughed at his jokes. TD had had a variety of follow-the-rules jobs, first in the military. "Had to give orders that got some of my men killed. Never got over that. Disability pension. Served as deck crew aboard cargo ships. No room for mistakes there either. All I did was risk my neck to make someone else wealthy. Screw it. Never got used to the foul-mouthed, anal humour of the mates I wound up with in either place so I graduated to this." He spread his arms to the sunshine, stream and waving forest beyond.

"About as succinct a resume as I ever heard," replied Jacob.

TD didn't wait to be asked if he wanted a second donut. "Well?" he asked, waving his new treat at his host.

Jacob introduced himself with both his names and then added a thumbnail life story, ending with his current position.

"We had to study historic battles as part of officer training. Always bugged me that the point of their stories was tactical not why they were there at all."

"You'd have been a great Diogenes."

"Heard that name somewhere - tell me about him." He raised an eyebrow as he looked at the survivors on the torn bag. Jacob pushed it over. TD was about to pick up a third when he looked past Jacob and held up a hand. "Hold that thought."

Jacob turned to see another vagrant pushing a loaded shopping cart along the walkway. TD called to him. "Pete. Got something for you."

Pete broke his fixation on his cart and looked up.

"Come over here. Got a treat for you. Jake here bought you breakfast but you have to share it with the others."

Pete swept the bag that was held out to him with a laser glance, flashed a glance at TD and scooped the package from him. He bundled the torn edges over the contents and stuffed the bag under a sleeping bag on top of a plastic bag bulging with beer cans. He muttered something inaudible towards Jacob and bowed over his cart again.

"Remember. You have to share. See you later," TD called as Pete was halfway through his turn. Pete muttered something to himself and resumed his plod onward.

"A head injury," TD explained. "A bunch of us hang out under the bridge downstream. Thanks for the rations. Now you were going to tell me about … "

Jacob did.

TD couldn't stop laughing at the story about the response Diogenes gave to Alexander the Great. "You know I can think of a General I wish I had said that to." And he slapped his thigh again. "That story is a keeper. I love that one. So, tell me more about this guy."

The next hour flashed by in conversation rarely heard outside an academic seminar. Towards the end, TD nodded towards the pencil and shavings still sitting on Jacob's notebook. Jacob had been sharpening it when TD had first approached.

Jacob nodded that he liked to use a pencil because he could more easily correct his mistakes. He got out his jack knife again. TD did the same and laid a weapon on the table beside Jacob's whittler.

"It was my Dad's. WW two. He was merchant marine." TD unfolded the marlin spike on the back of the tool. "For splicing rope," he explained. "Doubt you could find many who know how to do that now. I use it if I need to dig." He clasped the handle showing how easily it fit his hand. The round steel shone with use; the point was still strong.

The spike closed with a snap and he opened a blade that could make short work of a food can if you knew how to use it. Jacob recalled having a smaller but similar item in the kitchen of his childhood.

When TD closed the can opener and opened the single knife blade, it was a murderous weapon. Broad backed, keenly sharp, swiftly pointed - it was made for hard, even deadly work. TD handed it across. XL was etched into the base of the sturdy blade near the hinge. The cross-hatched bakelite grip filled Jacob's palm comfortably with the spike folded down.

"It's done a lot of work," Jacob said noticing the few black scratches. A sheen of oil on the surface caught the light. "You keep it well." He didn't need to test the edge on a page of his notebook. He knew it would sizzle through it effortlessly.

"Hmmm."

Over the summer, and through TD, Jacob met the community of homeless men who lived within sight of Lindsay Tower. All had their reasons for avoiding shelters, but it was plain that most were not living so much as they were trying not to die. They were stuck at the bottom of Maslow's Hierarchy. Their whole existence was absorbed in meeting their needs for food and shelter. Their animated philosophical discussions that Jacob had with the group over day-old donuts and cold coffee told how deeply and how aware these men were of the world as it was and as it could be. They had ideas and solutions and ribald jokes about why it wasn't their way. But it all disappeared ten steps from his table. Which soup kitchen was serving a dinner? What's the price on copper because one had found three discarded motors? See you later.

By summer's end he was resigned to the conclusion that what mattered was how he helped anyone he met. Their philosophy or practices really didn't matter. He felt more like Buddha or maybe Diogenes with a job. He'd just stop worrying about things as he had and drifted like the leaves that now fell into the stream and floated past toward their downstream destiny.

Instead of regaling visitors with the hair-splitting arguments he had learned, he took to buying his coffee in bulk at the coffee shop and offering those who stopped, a cup from the take-out box and an ear to talk to. So it was that Ezra found him again.

"I heard you were here. Well I guessed it had to be you. Nobody else would be talking about philosophers. That's what the talk is; that there is a modern-day Socrates under a big umbrella down by the river. You can get a coffee and talk all day to him if you want."

Jacob jumped up and shook his former student's hand till it fell off. He hadn't recognized him in colourful Spandex till Ezra took off his racing helmet and tinted glasses. "Coffee is what Diogenes would have used if he had it. Instead he was forced to use a lamp. Anyway, I'll take your story as a compliment." He dragged Ezra to the table. "My, it's wonderful to see you again. Sit down and tell me something. You'll be starting at your new school soon eh? Nice bike by the way."

Ezra gave him the specs on the bike - carbon composite frame, weight, gear ratios, how fast he'd gone on it. "As for school, I got into a place that has all their courses modularized and lets you work at your own pace. I've already started. It's a piece of cake. I fear my big problem will be keeping interested in what the syllabus offers."

"Suggestion? Remember that the teacher in charge may be smarter than they appear. You command the conversation if you ask the questions and they might appreciate someone with your critical thinking skills." Ezra seemed to consider the thought.

"How's your Mom doing?" Jacob continued.

"Seems happy doing investment counselling at a cross-town branch of the bank downstairs in the Tower. She's good at following rules and she has a great rapport with her conservative clients. Kept one couple from losing a bundle lately. They can't say enough about her. She passed some sort of review lately, so I guess she's on the team."

"And how about you and her. That working better?"

"Yeah, I guess. She still wants to know where I am all the time but I know she means well. I got some creds from pointing out the nasties to her one day and how I steered clear of them. She gave me a little slack after that ...and the bike."

"Hear from any of the other kids or parents?"

"That is the one topic that's got Mom a bit nervous." Ez went on to name two of his Mom's fellow graduates who had simply stopped responding to her calls in recent days. "Voicemail box is full. No bounce back responses from emails to say they were received. That sort of stuff."

"Lots of reasons for that happening," Jacob replied. "There are lots of places that have poor or no internet connections. Could be on assignment somewhere. Might be down with flu or just distracted with family. Been known to happen. In fact, I've decided to stop answering media messages myself. I use only audio contact. If they don't want to talk, I don't want to tweet."

"What is really burning up the wires is Miss Maggie's romance." Ez said and went on to elaborate on overheard exchanges from his Mom. "They seem to be cutting some sort of swath through the after-hours scene. Her name is Dallas. Don't know much about her but that." Jacob listened while his pupil recited a litany of parties topped off with the very expensive car that the lover was always seen driving.

Yawn thought Jacob but he kept his face straight and eyes fixed on Ez as though this news was earthshaking.

"Time for me to go," Ez announced rather abruptly. "I have some work I need to do for Co-op before Internet time tonight. I'll tell Mom you asked after her."

"Co-op going well?" Jacob asked trying to extend the contact.

"Great. You wouldn't believe what a great person Ms. Asa is to work with. That lady is something. Man does she know how to make that machinery dance." Ez snapped on his safety gear and disappeared behind his shades, now very much the athletic racer from a Tour de France clip.

"Hope to see you at the reunion?"

"Mom can't wait. Maybe I'll be able to come."

"I'd like to hear how school is going, whether all that critical thinking stuff I spent my time on was worth the trouble."

"OK, if you put it that way. See you then."

And away he went with a whiz of tires and a casual wave before he bent over the handlebars.

16

Networking was all Jacob heard about as he meandered about the Reunion. "You really have to culture those contacts you make during training," he heard more than one advise their sanctuary sisters. "You know when the boss asks you to get coffee for the group - you know what a downer that is? Well use it to find out where they get their coffee. Ask if they want nibbles to go with it. Talk to the supplier, ask about his job. You never know when you might need that name. Keep a book if you can't remember ..." Ezra's Mom pulled out a slim booklet to show names dates, places, emails and phone contacts, business cards for any connection she had made outside of the clients she had at the bank.

"You may have a job when you leave here but you can be adrift so fast ...". Jacob left as the conversation switched to the threats of the modern world of work.

Maggie swept into the room with her companion. The fashion plate caught the glances; Maggie caught the hugs. While Maggie greeted everyone by name, Dallas held back measuring each woman her lover hugged as if she was measuring the other woman for a suit.

"I have an announcement to make," Maggie said after the first flurry. "I think you all know Dallas," and she turned to smile broadly at her friend. Everyone smiled kindly but the room temperature dropped noticeably. "Dallas is taking over a job that has needed doing for a long time. She is starting a research program on the successes you all have achieved. We want to know what we are doing here that is working well and not. You could offer thoughts on what we should be adding to our program. She has already started contacting graduates from years ago and will be working her way through the Alumni list. It would be appreciated if you could help her assemble the data she wants to collect to make beneficial suggestions and design effective policies." Jacob noticed a few women sucked in a breath as their faces froze.

"But that is for days to come," Maggie continued. "Let us all share our time together tonight."

The sound level bounced up as groups digested the announcement. Maggie resumed her circuit trailing her new Director of Research. Jacob saw the young man he was looking for beside the table of hors d'oeuvre. Ez was talking to students about what was best on the plates but broke off to come and say hello. Jacob didn't have a chance to ask about his courses.

"Not one of my classmates can ask a question worth the trouble," Ez declared. They accept everything on paper as authority. Boy would it be easy to take over the world if everybody is like that." He continued on hardly taking a breath.

"So, you are doing well?" Jacob interrupted. "I get the feeling you like the job."

"This is so easy. And you were right about the teacher's knowing more than they seem." He was off to the races again. Enthusiasm bubbled out of him uncontrollably.

"You guys seem to be the success story everyone wants to hear about," Jacob commented. "I was listening to your Mom over there," he nodded across the room where the knot of women had expanded slightly and they were talking animatedly.

"Well I'm not sure about the other news," Ez intimated. "There are three who said for weeks they'd be here and they aren't. In each case they just seemed to disappear. There one day, not answering calls the next. Mom sent me around the room twice to see if they had arrived late. Nada!"

"Sounds like an unusual coincidence," Jacob admitted.

"Not all," Ez continued. "I was coming home late earlier in the week from the library. Waiting at a traffic light, I thought I spotted Her Majesty's car in an empty parking lot. I mean it is a one-of-a-kind car." He tipped his head towards the Research Director. "There was one other car in the lot and out of it got that woman, as the light changed. She had her head down and looked upset as she hurried to her car - not like she is now. Anyway, I followed your advice about listening to my intuition and wrote down that other car's license number." He pulled out his smart phone and pulled out post-it note from the inside cover. "You don't know how hard it is to find a pen and paper at my house," he said as he passed Jacob the note.

Jacob's pocket protector in the shirt pocket beneath his sport coat suddenly seemed heavy. The lump of his penknife pressed against his leg through his pocket. "I don't know if this is important or not, but I thought you'd know what to do."

Jacob accepted the note reluctantly. Here he was getting notes from a nosy parishioner again.

He filed it in his Day-Timer after making a note on it of its origin and significance and then a copy in his book, while Ez continued.

"Can we keep up our ice cream meetings?" Ez asked tentatively.

"You don't know how happy that would make me." Then in a response to a wave from his boss, he said to Ez, "I think your Mary is looking for you. She's looked this way twice while we were talking."

Ez turned to recognize the smile. "See you Saturday, at 3, there?"

"Done."

Ez strode away as Maggie and her companion cornered him against the column.

If I could just wiggle sideways to the hatch doorway, I could be out of sight before ..., he thought but too late.

"Dallas, I'd like you to meet Jacob Eiger, the philosophy teacher in our school," Maggie said.

Jacob assumed the clerical voice and interested half smile from a million previous meetings without even thinking. "So good to meet you Ms ...?

"Quinn," she replied. Her handshake was firm; her eyes sharpened to try to penetrate his facade.

"Tell me about the research project," Jacob opened. It had the desired effect of drawing out a plan to interview each person who had passed through the program Maggie had created and collect answers in a bunch of questionnaires. "There will be many factors that have to be eliminated in evaluating whether the results are cause or coincidental." She smiled benignly. She rattled on about medians and margins of error for a while.

"Can statistics create a one-size-fits-all program, do you think?" The question seemed to catch her off guard.

"Well that is one of the possible results - to see if some activities or interventions are applicable to all or to particular groups." She rattled on about sample size and parameters, variables and statistical significance.

Sounds like Bullshit to me, he thought but he said, "That sounds like such an interesting way to apply analysis to such a serious social problem." He wrinkled brow was flawless.

"Have you already started your interviews?" he continued when all she did by reply was smile.

"Well underway," she said. "Everyone has been so co-operative in setting aside time for me. I do most of the interviews after their workdays, you know."

"My goodness, based on all those questionnaires, you must be busy a lot of nights."

"Oh, only about two or three a week now, but that will pick up. I'd like to have all my data to take on a vacation. Maggie and I are planning a Cuban getaway. She smiled knowingly and gave a little shiver. "Well I'll get there early and do most of the analysis then she'll join me just before or just after Christmas."

"Have you met with …" he recited the three names Ez had mentioned earlier? "I only ask because I had hoped to meet them here again." He didn't mention that they had moved out of the Tower community years before he arrived.

"Why yes. They were among my first. In fact, I saw Liya, I think it was yesterday as I recall … and she was headed off on holiday." We had to squeeze in the meeting when we did for that reason. When Jacob guided the conversation to those with the others, she ticked off the plausible reasons for their absence that he had imagined like factors in a formula.

"Well maybe I'll see them next time," Jacob said.

Dallas seemed to catch a signal from Maggie. "I see I'm being called. So nice to meet you Mr. ….?"

"Eiger - like the mountain," he replied.

She smiled and nodded. *They said he was aloof and out of touch. No wonder, with a name like that,* she thought.

Jacob admired the retreating form, which seemed to add a more seductive sway, assuming he was watching. Well he was, and he did notice. *Did you ever get too old to not notice,* he wondered?

He spotted Maggie's personal secretary conversing with the caterer seeming to suggest he remove some moth-eaten plates. Zorina recognized him as he approached. "Dinner will be shortly Sir," she said.

"I'm looking forward to it. I have a question which I wondered if you could help me with. I was wondering about inviting Maggie and friend to Solstice dinner at my house so I wondered if you knew off hand, when business will wrap up for the holidays.

"Well they're going off for holidays in Cuba at right after the Solstice Celebration here."

"I guess I better extend my invitation either before or after," Jacob said and smiled.

"Dinner is served," called the caterer.

17

"Here she comes again," said the doorman to the valet at the casino. "Right on schedule." He checked his watch. 9:20.

"Jeez, that is one set of wheels," the valet admired. He was new. "You say she comes here a lot?"

"Two, maybe three times a week. Wait till you see the skirt. Treat her like royalty. This lady is one big spender. Tips big if she wins … which isn't often. Even if she doesn't, she pays your salary and mine every night."

The sports car swept to the door and the driver stepped out, smoothed her skirt and then with a smile tossed the key to the valet.

"Buena suerte," he said, then corrected himself. "Good Luck," the valet wished her.

The lady ignored the comment and strode through the door, held wide for her.

"Hey man," the valet said to the doorman as he gave the older man his smart phone. "Take my picture with me and that car before I park it." Both checked that the lady was out of sight. Click.

"Ven aqui. Selfie," he said again. A quick glance. Nobody coming. The two posed beside the car. Click. The valet laughed all the way to the lot. *I'm sending that home and tell them it's my new car,* he thought.

When she stormed out, right on schedule an hour and a half later, she did not tip either employee.

18

Being so attractive made her an easy mark, the enforcer thought as he sat in the car. Simply threaten that pretty face or that show-stopping figure and she'd agree to do whatever he 'asked'. Now that she had racked up some big debts, it was not hard to convince her to pay them off with her special accesses. But he wasn't the one to do the talking. His boss was in the back seat and so was the target.

That's all she was - a means to an end. She had access to a very wealthy employer's accounts and to a host of marketable clients that could be trafficked easily. His boss was making the demands clear as he watched the discussion through his rearview mirror. He couldn't hear anything because of the armour glass separation but it was plain the lady didn't like the terms of repaying the debts she'd piled up.

The lady quickly burst out of the back seat and slammed the door and bolted for her car.

Be careful, dearie. That sort of behaviour could get you a reaction you didn't expect, he thought.

The boss in the back seat only pointed forward. He started the car and turned towards the parking lot entrance. He let the cyclist at the intersection go through the light first as it changed. No point in attracting attention by cutting off the kid.

As he drove his smart phone clamped on the dashboard chimed quietly. Three addresses appeared with times beside each. He'd get the team, collect the clients, and deliver each to the warehouse for processing. *Easy week's work*, he thought.

19

Ez spotted Jacob crossing the street headed to the Mall where they were to meet for ice cream. He wheeled into the crosswalk and followed his former teacher across, dismounting from his bike as he did.

Jacob jumped at the clacking sound of cycling shoes just as Ez suddenly appeared beside him. "Here I was hoping you'd be late and I'd get to eat it all myself," Jacob joked.

"That is an excellent reason for being on time, I think." Ez replied. "I asked if Mary could join us but she said she could only do so if we met on Sundays. She works down the Mall but is usually finished late afternoon."

"It's OK with me," Jacob agreed as they walked.

"Well it's fine with me. I'll set it up for next week?" Ez said then stopped suddenly. The front wheel of his bike turned to abruptly cut off Jacob from going forward.

"Look over the cars," Ez directed. "That big guy headed for the black sedan. The lights just flashed. Is that the license number I gave you back at the party?"

Jacob noted the man and the car but was distracted by the request for the note Ez had given him. "Ezra don't ask a senior a question like that. Yes, I have the note still but I haven't done anything with it. I certainly don't recall the number."

Ez was muttering to himself as he pulled out his smart phone. "Damn. Sorry Sir. I'm out of power."

Jacob flipped open his Day-Timer to the week separated by an elastic band from the rest, found the note and read it out to Ez. It was getting smeared. He was glad he'd written the details more clearly in the space.

"That's it," said Ez. "That is the car I saw Ms. Dallas getting out of. And that guy that just got into the driver's seat is the brute in the Food Court we thought was a mobster."

The luxury car drove past them down the next aisle of the lot. Two cars were already moving into the space he had left.

"Are you saying he met Ms. Quinn last week?"

"No No. He was driving. If he were in the car, I'd bet he was the driver. Ms. Dallas would have been talking to his boss in the back seat."

Jacob looked at Ezra full on. "Are you saying Ms. Quinn is consorting with people you think are gangsters?"

Ez's excitement melted immediately. He heaved a sigh. "Well, everybody knows that man is a mobster and I saw her in this boss's company and she was upset as a result. How does it add up to you?"

"First off, I don't know he's a mobster, and I didn't see her. So, I at least must reserve judgment. It's a really awful accusation to make. Why in the world would our senior exec's companion be seeing a mob boss? I think you are enjoying an overworked imagination. Stop there. Talk to me about your classes or something else."

Ez was plainly deflated. He realized he'd gone off half-cocked. "You go to the ice cream place. I'm going in through the bank door to drop my bike where Mary says it will be safe. I'll meet you in a few minutes."

As Jacob made his way to the appointment place, he noted as usual, the Art Supply display, and as he crossed the corner of the Food Court, that the table where the large man was usually scowling, was vacant. *Well of course,* he thought. *He just drove out of the parking lot. But is being big, and scowling and taking up two parking spaces in the lot, a crime? If 'everybody' knows he's a criminal, why isn't he behind bars? Case closed.*

"Yes," Jacob replied to the server at the counter. "I'll have the largest piece of Creamy Coffee Ice Cream

Pie the law allows and a double David Harum for my friend coming shortly."

"That will be ..." the server said with a smile.

20

Jacob maintained his contact with TD even as the weather changed towards winter. It was just too cold to sit at the picnic table by the river anymore. They met at the donut shop where he'd met Maggie. Meeting Ez on the weekend and TD in midweek, gave secure bookends between which to organize the rest of his time not involved at school. Life settled into a comfortable rhythm.

At one of the first indoor gatherings, Winston joined the bunch. He was the guy who'd found the motors being cleared out of a warehouse and had subsequently returned to the place to see if anything else of value was in the trash. On this particular night when the talk was about where to sleep was on everyone's mind, he said that there was room for a couple in a storeroom inside the warehouse. The place was abandoned; he'd found a broken window he said. It was out of the weather and he figured he had his winter digs till that day.

The place had previously had two small manufacturing outfits. Both had died. He had been wakened that day by noise in the other end of the building. Three big house trailers had been rolled into that part. He'd seen them through nail holes in the partition that separated his space from the other.

Later some noise drew him back to the peep hole again just in time to see a bunch of guys carrying or holding up staggering women as they were taken into the trailers. He thought a couple were handcuffed. And then just before he'd come over, there was the most almighty screaming came out of that end. Sounded like first one woman then another was being beat up. It all calmed down after a while but what did the others think? Should he continue to sleep there with all the racket? Would it attract attention and an investigation that would find him?

"Get out of Dodge," said one. "You don't want to be there when the fuzz arrives. They make your life miserable."

"You say you saw women? How many?" asked TD.

"Three or four."

"Between the horses that brought the trailers leaving and the women arriving, there was this big black car came in driven by a guy as big as a house. Mean looking bugger. He left after a short while. That's when the noise started up.

Jacob's heart stopped at the description of the driver of the big black car.

Jacob spoke up to ask if he happened to get the black car's license number. That brought loud guffaws from the rest of the table. "I wasn't going to buy it," Winston laughed and everyone joined in the joke - but Jacob.

*

It was between classes and he was catching up on voicemail messages. It was the urgent one from the bank to which he was responding. Banking and finance were not Jacob's strengths. Margaret used to look after all that. He just couldn't get into the competitive spirit to monitor money and squeeze out advantages from other people. All this cluttered his mind as the phone rang through.

"Mr. Eiger", said the bank employee after he had identified himself. "Thank-you for calling back so promptly. I reached out earlier to say that your account will be overdrawn if we pay out your mortgage payment today."

"I don't understand. How can that be? My pay cheque covers that easily."

"That's just it. Your paycheque hasn't arrived for two months. We thought you might have quit your job."

Jacob was stunned. The silence stretched until the clerk said, "Sir, are you still there?"

"I'll get back to you before lunch. Can you hold the payment till this afternoon?"

There was an off-phone muttering that ended with, "We will have to hear from you before three."

His next call was to accounting and the line was busy. He took the stairs down, two at a time, and found he could not get onto the floor. He had to go to the ground floor, back through the lobby and up in the elevator. When he entered the accounting office, the calm and business-like atmosphere tingled with static as though a thunderstorm was about to break. The secretary saw him and simply handed him a form. "Fill this in," she directed and turned back to the phone that had not stopped ringing.

"We're not sure if we've had a cyber-attack or if the accounting program just collapsed. Your paycheque will be in your account by noon," said the secretary as she collected his form and added it to a stack of similar ones.

"I've missed two cheques," he said over the insistent ringing of the phone again.

"Did you put that on your form?" She plucked it from the pile. "Here, write in the first pay that was missed." She all but threw the form at him and snapped a pen down beside it. He did as he was told and waved the form to get her attention. She took it from him, mouthed a harried *thank-you*, and turned back to her call.

As he was waiting for the elevator, he called the bank with the news. An announcement over the Public Address system advised all that a meeting would be held after school in the Lounge. He didn't have to guess what the topic was.

When he reached the lounge later, the spectrum ran from sullen silence to hysteria. Teachers, cleaning staff, clerical workers were all in clumps talking about relatives overseas who were suddenly not receiving the payments that kept them from destitution, credit card payments that had bounced, groceries that had to be left at the store when the debit cards were declined.

Maggie, the Heads of Accounting, HR, and the Legal Department had their heads together in the corner. Maggie turned and called for everyone's attention. "I'm so sorry for all the distress this problem has caused," she began when the room quieted. "At present, we are not sure how the payroll program failed if it was attacked or simply broke down. The fact that the program has served well for years and has happened over two cycles makes us think there has been an outside infiltration. All salaries have been replaced from reserve funds and should already be in your accounts. If there are particular problems you have experienced, please speak to Human Resources." She motioned towards the various Department Heads who had spread out to different tables around the room.

The meeting broke up with most heading for the elevators, expressing relief; some were walking towards the tables with staff before she stopped talking.

Jacob waited till Maggie had talked to those with more pressing needs than his before he approached her. "I wonder if we could talk in your office for a few minutes?" he asked.

"If it's about your pay, you …" He cut her off abruptly. "No, it is another matter. It needs … I need to run something past you. I think it's important."

"Could it wait till tomorrow? It has been a hard day."

"No. This needs to be talked about now."

"Ok, she sighed. "Let's go down."

In her office, Maggie sagged onto the sofa; Jacob chose to stand and pace. "I'm afraid you might react badly but I have to say what's on my mind because I'm the only one who has this information." He was standing at the window looking out.

"I've received information from three sources that Ms. Quinn may not be who she seems." Maggie's head snapped up as he turned around. Her eyes were flashing.

He held up his hands, "Please hear me out. This is serious. I want no harm to come to you but every intuitive bell I have is clanging off the hook. Please just listen."

Maggie slouched back and pinched her lips.

"I spoke to her when she came to the reunion. She tried to give me a snow job. In particular, she claims to be applying statistical methods to her study of graduates. I've done a bit of statistics as part of my studies of archeological evidence. What she told me made me wonder if she knows a standard deviation from a decimal." Maggie leaned forward to get up. "There's more. Please let me continue."

"Three women who had been in touch and were counting on coming to the reunion, didn't show up. The reasons offered by Ms, Quinn were entirely too glib. And all three seem to have disappeared after being interviewed by Ms. Quinn as part of the research project." He held up his hands again.

"Further, Ms. Quinn was seen getting out of the back of a car driven by someone who was later seen in the warehouse district in a deserted warehouse - well deserted except for a couple large house trailers hidden inside. Some think this guy is a gangster. Shortly after he left, horrific women's screams were heard coming from those trailers." The smouldering eyes never left him.

"And then there was today. Everything is working well. She arrives and they don't. When I try to connect these dots, the lines cross through Ms. Quinn."

Maggie rose like a thundercloud. "You make the most insulting accusations about a fellow staff member and impugn my judgment, not to mention making oblique comments about my personal life. You have stepped way past the line. Eiger, get out now." She was shaking with fury.

Jacob stepped quickly to the door. He opened it and turned back. "Here's the license number of the car she got out of and which another thinks was driven by a thug. Please look into it." He laid the smudged post-it on the table beside the door. When he looked up, she was reaching for the coffee table in front of her. He quickly stepped out and had just closed the door when something heavy crashed against it.

*

He didn't sleep. Well past midnight, he paged back through his Day-Timer to a business card taped to the page for the day he had rescued Brian. The detective had told him to call any time. He did.

"Please leave a message," a robotic voice growled.

"Detective Winters, it's Jacob Eiger calling. You gave me your card when you were investigating the case of a student whose father suited him up with a suicide vest and sent him back to his Mom where he was supposed to blow up. You told me to call anytime." He gave the time. "I think I have tripped over a serious crime and don't know who to tell about it. Would you call back please," and he read out his mobile phone number."

Before he was back from the bathroom, his phone was ringing.

"Private caller" announced the screen. He punched it on hopefully.

A sleepy voice said, "Mr. Eiger?"

"Yes?"

"Detective Winters here. I'm retuning your call."

Jacob let out a sigh and sat down on the edge of his bed.

"I don't know what else to do. I think I have pieces of a puzzle that describes a serious crime. I told my boss about it and that may have got me fired. That still would leave those involved in maybe a life-threatening situation. I needed to share it with you who might better …" He faded off.

"What is the crime, you think you have information about?"

"I'm no lawyer but from what I know, it may involve assault, maybe theft.

"Ok let's hear what you have," Winters's voice was clear now and all business.

Jacob poured out his story.

"Please repeat that license number again," asked Winters.

"And who were the eyewitnesses?"

"I'd rather not share that at the moment. Can you still go ahead and ask?"

"Well we get a lot of anonymous tips and it isn't as though we're looking for things to do especially at this hour."

"Please do two things and if you need to know the witness's names, I'll speak to them to come to you. Please look into that license number and the warehouse."

"The license is easy. I could also send a car by the warehouse. What's the address?"

"I only know the details of the place not its address." He described what he knew.

"Well that probably applies to many places."

"Could you look up recently bankrupt manufacturers, one of which had a bunch of motors needed for their process?"

"Know anyone who doesn't use motors in manufacturing?"

"Computer geeks, book publishers, storage places? And there would be two businesses with almost the same address. The place would be within easy walking distance of the donut store near the Lindsay Tower."

Winters sighed, "I'll look into it."

"Could you call me back?"

"Look, if there is anything I need further, I'll call. If you don't hear, we probably could not act. I can't divulge information from an investigation."

"Fair enough. But please hurry."

Dead air.

Jacob next called the school office and left an excuse on the voicemail that he was ill and did not want to bring any illness he might have, to school today. The students should continue with their assignments. Then, despite the hour, he dressed warmly and headed through the pre-dawn grey for the donut shop.

Down the street, the men's shelter required all overnight residents to be out by eight. It was almost nine before Jacob recognized one of the street people he knew from the summer.

"I need to get in touch with TD or Winston," he said. "Do you know where they might be?" Of course, he didn't. "If you see him, I'll be here till dinner. I really need to see either or both of them. It's important."

"Yer, the prfessr, aren't yah. You fed us coffee and donuts all summer down to the stream."

"Yeah."

"I'll pass the werd."

Both showed up before lunch. They moved down the street to the Best Burger Palace where he paid for doubles and fries.

*

"Well I can't go back there," moaned Winston. He looked haggard, - bloodshot eyes and trembling hands - worse than Jacob had ever seen him. He went on at length about being awakened by the flash of light through the window as the patrol car swung off the street into the driveway of the warehouse. When it didn't leave, he suspected the worst, scooped up his stuff and bailed out.

"I kept the shipping containers and stack of pallets between me and the place. To get round the corner. Just as well. More damned police cars than a bloody parade. Been walking since then. Don't know where to go tonight." He looked down at his empty plate.

"There's the shelter..." began Jacob.

"No bloody way. They've got bedbugs. Those critters get into your stuff and you got them forever. And some of those guys are crazy - shouting and hollering all night. No thanks."

Jacob looked up at TD who simply shrugged.

Maslow's Hierarchy of Needs popped up from deep in Jacob's memory. Shelter and food - which was first? Diogenes living in a barrel. The silence stretched out. Academics meet the real world. Oh well. He pulled over his serviette and wrote on it. "You can stay at my place," he said and slid the address across the table. "It's warm and out of the weather. But you have to put up with me."

Winston looked at the serviette. "You snore?" he asked as he raised his eyes. There was a tired smirk at the corner of his mouth.

"Yes. But you'll have your own bloody room." Jacob burst out, then realized he'd been jerked around. He was surprised at himself, swearing like that. He leaned back and chuckled, "I doubt you'll hear me." Then he returned the gruff manner, "Do you?"

"Do I what?"

"Snore?"

"No."

"Good," said Jacob. "And you don't smoke do you? You can't come if you smoke, even outside."

"Not a smoker," assured Winston.

"So next item is Detective Winters. He's is going to want to talk to you."

"Not going to happen," replied Winston. "If that is the price of staying at your house. I'll sleep in the street."

"He just wants you to identify the big guy who was the driver, tell what you saw when the women arrived."

"That old four-letter word again. I'm not going to 'just' do anything. I have a history with police that will not be repeated."

"Jacob," interrupted TD. "You'll have to convince Winters to say he found the warehouse by an anonymous tip. He rescued the women. He can question the thugs he found on site. Winston is not going to get involved. End of story."

Jacob pinched up a lettuce fragment that had escaped his burger while he mentally organized the rest of his day. "Ok, I have something else to do. Winston, I'll see you for dinner at my place if you want chili. I'll be back about six. Thanks for what you did for those women. TD, can we still do the weekly coffee thing with any who wants to?"

"Sure."

"Just don't want to lose touch."

"No problem."

Winston tentatively raised a hand to interrupt the farewell. "I want to be sure I understand you clearly. You said you'd be back for dinner about six and you said I could join you for chili?"

"Yes," Jacob said as he reached for his coat.

"But the meal at six is supper not dinner. You want me to be at your place for supper?"

"Yeah. I want you there at six. If you call it supper, that's what it will be but it still will be chili."

"Ok."

"See you then." Jacob tucked in his scarf and zipped his coat. He made sure the earflaps were down on his hat. He waved at the server as he left. He'd have to go home before his next appointment.

21

"I am here to offer spiritual support to Ms. ..." Jacob had his Day-Timer in hand and he referred to it for the name. "Ms. Monette. She was admitted last night." The information clerk checked her database and gave the floor and room number. "Elevator's that way on the left." she pointed.

Walking down the hallway, he resisted the urge to stretch his clerical collar that seemed too tight. That it was still in the back of his sock drawer at all must have been an Act of God. He had to smile at that. Even though he was retired, he was officially on the list of those who would do substitutions or short-term assignments and because of that he was still licensed by his old denomination. It was just a specific congregation that had sent him packing. His black suits, cleaned and bagged, were at the end of the rail in his closet. They were still serviceable; he'd just not intended to use them again. Until today.

"Go ahead, Father," said a young lady stepping aside as the elevator door opened.

The invitation caught him by surprise. He smiled his most beatifically towards her and stepped ahead.

The nurse at the station pointed him to a 4-bed room on the ward when he asked, "I'm substituting for Ms. Maggie until she can get here personally," he explained to the blank face that stared up from the sheets. "I'm Jacob Eiger. I teach in the school."

"I know your name. I was hoping to meet you. Everybody talks about your classes with the kids."

"How are you feeling?"

"Good as can be expected. I guess. I think they were drugging me." The conversation continued quietly about her rescue and the food.

"Can you tell me how you were abducted?" he asked. "I presume you were following all the precautions you learned."

"It happened right after I talked to Ms. Quinn. She asked me all those questions and I did more on her laptop. I guess it took about a half an hour. I was surprised it went so fast. She left and a few minutes later there was a tap on the door. I opened it thinking she had come back because she forgot something. There were these two guys there. They pushed me back, knocked me down and I felt this sting in my arm. That's all I remember till I felt sort of cold and was being held up as I crossed a parking lot. My feet wouldn't work right. I kept stumbling but someone was holding me up. I felt terrible - like I wanted to throw up and dazed. Like I was sleep-walking."

"Everybody thought you were going on a holiday."

"Holidays are for people who can afford them. I'm not in that league for a while. I was hoping to get a down payment together for a condo. A go-away holiday is on the other side of that goal."

"I don't want to wear you out and it is time for me to be elsewhere," Jacob said eventually.

"I'm glad you came. This is a boring place to be."

"Get well soon," Jacob wished her, and made his exit.

*

The next day's newspapers carried the story of a human trafficking ring that had been broken. Five kidnapped women rescued. By then Jacob had talked to two of the three who had not come to the reunion. Both had just spoken to the new Director of Research who had just left. A few minutes later, the timid knock on the door and Bang!

Jacob felt he had to relay this to Maggie but was not sure how. He was definitely persona non grata in her office. But maybe Zorina could help. He called.

"I don't know what you said to Ms. Maggie but it set off a lot of broken stuff in her office," Zorina confessed.

"Well leave her the locations of the women. Maybe she'll drop by on the weekend. They'd love to see her."

"I doubt she'll be out of the office. The financial problems that screwed up the payroll seem to have expanded into the investment and endowment funds. When they put a lockdown on any fund transfers they didn't put bank drafts on that list. Since then there have been a rash of them issued …"

"What's a bank draft?"

"Well it takes money out of an account and puts it in limbo till the bearer cashes it. Then the money comes out of wherever and into the new account. Anyway, if the scurry is any measure of the amount of the missing money, it is substantial."

So, someone has a bunch of drafts and then cashes them into their own account?"

"Yeah, that's the short version."

"Does the bank know if they were cashed yet?"

"Well they know they haven't been even though some were issued over a month ago."

"Hope it all gets straightened away by the holiday season. Aren't Maggie and Dallas headed off for a holiday?... Cuba was it?"

"Still on the books from September. Tickets and rooms all arranged. Did you arrange your dinner before they leave? You were going to, I thought."

"Ewww. I was going to do that, wasn't I? I forgot. Maybe now is not a good time to send an invite. I've been off sick last day or so. I'll be back for class after the weekend - if I haven't received a dismissal notice."

"Well it was close but you haven't been terminated yet," Zorina said. "I'd hate to see you go."

"Ok, I wonder if you could pass along some information to Maggie. I went to see ... "and he relayed the results of his chats with the reunion absentees."

"Well there's nothing left to break in her office. Maybe I could do that?" she joked.

"Ms. Dallas still in the office?"

"Saw her earlier, you want me to transfer you."

"NO thanks," he said too loudly.

Zorina laughed.

"No that's all for now."

"Good to talk to you. I'll pass along your messages."

"Bye."

*

"Mom says she has an appointment after work this week, to talk to Ms. Quinn for her research project," Ezra offered as they waited for their ice cream orders on Sunday afternoon. The news made Jacob take a deep breath.

"Seems funny to have sundaes on Sunday," quipped Mary.

"Is that a problem?" Ez asked, surprised at Jacob's reaction. Jacob was reaching for his wallet.

"He's surprised at what a sundae costs," Mary interjected.

They picked up their treats and headed towards a table.

"I see our friend is missing again," Ez observed. His table sat vacant across the eating area.

Jacob sat. "Tell me about what you're doing," he invited.

They did. As Jacob listened, he pegged Ezra as headed for a doctorate. Mary could apply for forensic auditing if she stuck the course. She sure had the instincts.

"Your turn," Ez said. He'd hardly touched his dessert. Jacob was finished his.

"Well I have a boarder for the time being anyway. He's homeless. With winter coming, he needed a place to stay. He's one of my summer students." Both kids laughed at the euphemism.

Did you hear about the kidnapped women this week?

Both said they had.

"You remember at the reunion that your Mom sent you looking for three women who were supposed to be there and weren't?"

"Yeah."

"All three were in the group that was rescued."

"Holy Smoke," breathed Ez. He was looking across the court at the vacant table.

"I'm going to suggest you talk to your Mom and … maybe tell her it might be better if she not be available for her interview with Ms. Quinn. I don't want to give you my reasons but whatever she wanted to talk about will keep."

Ezra said nothing as he looked across the food court. "You think Ms. Quinn is involved in the kidnapping of those women, don't you?" Ez finally said.

"I didn't say that and don't want you to either. There is no evidence of that. Don't leap to unwarranted conclusions."

Ez just looked at him.

"Anyway, time for me to go. With my boarder, I committed to making dinner - sorry supper. Dinner is at noon to him. It's M&C fortified with hamburger and a garden salad. A glass of white wine is recommended - it says it goes well with that menu right on the bottle. He got up.

"I'll go back with Mary. I left my bike in her office," Jacob said.

"Next week?"

"You're on."

"Be sure you tell your Mom."

"I will."

*

The pink telephone message slip was in his mailbox at school on top of the pile of administrivia. "Ez asks you to call," it said. The number was below. He pasted it into his Day-Timer.

Probably wants to change ice cream time, Jacob thought as he called, and then that other advisory came back to him.

"Did you tell your Mom?" Jacob said as soon as Ez answered.

"Yes, and here's more bearing on the subject. Did you know that Ms. Quinn is planning to skip the country soon?"

"How do you know that?"

"Never mind. I'm telepathic. Did you know?"

"From what I hear, she and Maggie have had a Christmastime getaway planned for months. Cuba, as I recall. A lot of issues have raised such a trip as a good idea lately."

There was a pause. "No, it's Cayman Islands."

"No. It's Cuba."

"NO," came the emphatic response. "It's Cayman. I see a charge for a single open ticket, Business Class, booked last ... Thursday."

Jacob got a sick feeling. That was the day he'd visited Liya in hospital. *Well at least I know where the info came from,* he thought.

"She also seems to be driving around a lot," Ez continued, "Lots of gasoline purchases from one station in particular - named station ..." he rhymed off the number and brand name. Wednesdays look like a favourite, usually late - ten till midnight. Jacob wrote the details in his notebook.

"Thanks."

22

"Tell me what gets men like you out on the streets and keeps them there?" Jacob asked that night at dinner.

"Why?"

"I work in the school in the Lindsay Tower. It is a safe haven for women that are escaping abuse of various kinds. They usually arrive with kids and those children fill up the school where I work. I've talked with the person who runs it and she says there are plans for a men's tower across the parking lot but someone would have to make a case for it. I want to know if such a place would be useful for men around here and you are at hand to ask."

"Well I can't say I'd be interested. I mean I like this place. The rules are pretty easy and nobody argues about the TV program. I can't remember the week I've eaten so well. It would be good to have my own spot. One room would do. I get by on a pension cheque because I don't have rent and what goes with it, to pay. As soon as you have an apartment, you have a utility bill on top of the TV that you need to see who wants to buzz through the door at the lobby. There's a big fridge and cupboards that need to be filled and emptied and refilled and it just seems like too damned much bother. You need a collection of pots and pans and dishes and towels and bedding," he was ticking them off on his fingers, "and a laundry schedule because Suzie Q has to do her laundry after eight so you have to do yours before. It just goes on and on."

"There's that four-letter word again."

Winston laughed, "Exactly."

"Well if you could get a job and earn a buck, you could buy coffee …"

"Why? Someone like you will buy me one, or I can pick one up free at the Shelter if I wanted. I'd buy you one there except I don't want you to get bedbugs. Lots of places to sit around and chew the fat - without coffee."

"Who cares? What's the point?"

"Exactly. We're all just waiting to die. You could enjoy the time and places you have or you can wear yourself out working and wishing for somewhere else for whatever reason. Just makes for a lot of unhappy people."

"What would you do if someone asked you for help?"

"Give it to them if I could. Why? You need help?

"Everybody needs help."

"Are you saying you want the place painted over the winter?" Winston looked at the walls and ceiling.

Jacob ignored the diversion. "Suppose Pete was ill and needed to go to Toronto. Would you earn the money that would get him there?"

"Well I could likely get him there but not the way you're thinkin'. And your point is what would we do to help each other? Well maybe the help that people really need isn't always, or even necessarily, the help that comes from the capital system that is running the store at the moment. I was there once. I got burned for life when I did what I thought was right even if it made me a criminal in the eyes of the law."

"It's similar for many I know on the street. Some have circuits burned out by drugs or accidents. Others arrived that way because of cruelty generations ago, but they all have many skills and contacts that are not valued by the systems that say they want to 'treat' them." His hooked fingers hung in the air a moment.

"So, to answer your question. I'd chose to do a lot. That you gave me a place here without a word of what you wanted in return, makes me think you're on the same path."

Jacob sat in stunned silence. Here was some vagrant actually living what Diogenes and all those ancients he had been studying were actually talking about. Well maybe. How can you believe what was written about anybody without taking a degree in linguistics?

"I'm glad we met," Jacob said eventually. "Can we talk more about this later? I hope you'll stay through till Spring at least."

"You sound like the third act of La Bohème,"

"What? You mean the opera? How do you know that?"

"Sang in it a couple times - chorus. Ever sing in an opera?"

Jacob looked down at his hands. He'd had led such a confined and sterile life. Here was a social outcast who could sing opera, who lived a philosophy idealized in academia and in the abstract and who was sharing insight with whom? *Why did I imagine I could help anyone else?* he wondered.

23

Jacob returned to class on Monday to find the staff nervous. Maybe it was the fact that senior staff, who usually were around and had a smile, were not seen at all. Their secretaries were constantly busy also. They too wore frowns instead of their customary smiles.

When the chance came, he called Detective Winters to thank him for rescuing the women.

He had to leave a message explaining also that the source that took him to the warehouse would not talk to him. Winters would have to explain it as an anonymous source.

The gas station with the number Ez had given him was quite a way out of town. He couldn't imagine why she would drive that distance to get gas. The station bragged of being a 'full service' station. He had to ask one of his students what that meant.

"They put the gas in for you so you don't have to get out of your car," a teenager told him.

Jacob returned to the website to find out where it was exactly. A convenient map showed the location marked by a red dot on a pin at an intersection. The map also showed a title of the adjoining convenience store. The map offered directions for how to get there and a travel time - not quite half an hour. Why would anyone drive past a dozen other stations to get gas way out there?

He tapped on the icon to show the place on a larger scale map. It backed out; roads shrank; town names jumped up. A large park was identified, and ... Ha! The Diamond Rock Casino. That car of hers probably passed everything but a gas station. She filled up either on the way to or from the Casino. But how did she get there without anybody knowing? If she were a gambler, surely that would be grist for the office gossip mill. And Ez said she was there on ...Wednesdays frequently. Those were nights she said she often did appointments. But they only lasted half an hour, Liya said. The timing could allow her maybe an hour or so at the casino?

Of course, his reasoning was threadbare at best. He knew that. It was exactly what got him tossed out of Maggie's office in the first place. Maybe he did have it in for Ms. Quinn and he just couldn't let it go. He moaned about it to Winston at supper.

"It's the fact that money is missing from a business that does good work to save a lot of women who would be destitute and victimized otherwise," he complained. "That's what really bugs me. And the losses coincide with her arrival," Jacob summarized.

"And where did all that concern get you?" Winston asked.

"Almost lost my job. I also got to run around another circle as sketchy as the first."

"Must be something better to do."

"Hmmm."

24

The Coffee Club of Dispossessed People was asked to leave the Donut Store. "You drive away the other customers," the owner complained. But he was amenable to giving Jacob a BOGO deal on cardboard carafes and cups if he took them off site. The group convened along the rim of the abutments that led down to the walkway along the water. They all thanked Jake and toasted his donation to the group's health. The carafes were barely empty before they were squashed flat into pads to insulate one of the men from the cold concrete

"Hey, it's still warm," he joked. Ribald jokes followed before chat cycled to who was hiring or who was missing.

Jacob had drawn two cups and was glad to see he'd not guessed wrongly as Pete turned the corner and headed their way slowly pushing his shopping cart overloaded with bags of cans and returnable bottles, sleeping bag on top. Pete nodded his thanks and blew steam from the brew before he sipped carefully. "Good to see you Pete," Jacob said. "How you doing?"

"Ok." He blew on another sip. "This is nice," he said.

The others greeted him cordially and Pete nodded to each in return but he didn't say anything.

"I heard you were wondering if your Researcher connected to the casino," TD said as people were preparing to depart.

"Winston must have put you on to that," Jacob said. "I have to give that one up. I'm trying to make the lady into a scapegoat to explain what's tearing up the place at work. There is some sort of financial disaster that has happened. A lot of money has gone missing - 'like WOW', to coin a phrase."

"Well you probably won't be interested in this picture I got from a friend who works in the kitchen at Diamond Rock. One of the valets was bragging about his new car." He called up a photo on his phone and passed it across to Jacob.

"The word is that she's a pretty big spender and the staff look forward to seeing her. Wednesday nights seem to be her favourite. Arrives after nine thirty, at least before ten most weeks."

It took Jacob a moment to figure out the photo on the phone in the bright daylight. When he did his jaw dropped.

TD continued on, "I've only seen one person driving a car like that. The scuttlebutt from the staff seems to be that she's quite a handsome woman and likes short skirts. Pretty arrogant too."

"Can you send this picture to me?" Jacob asked.

"Give me your email."

Jacob did reluctantly. *There goes my resolution just to talk to people,* he thought

"Done."

*

"Mom rebooked her appointment with Ms Quinn for after the holidays. She told her she had a lot of year-end business to look after this month and with the holidays… so it will happen in January." Ez said over the last of his ice cream.

"Detective Winters got back to me on Friday. He must have been tidying up his inbox before the weekend He'd done a search on that big car that our absent friend," he tipped his head to the vacant table across the food court, was driving. It was a long-term lease from a local dealership to a local business named Talent Enterprises. All above board. They arrange for bit actors and supernumeraries etc. to do video commercials - sort of like an agency for the video business. The script writers for commercials contact them for people to fill background roles, dress up like someone else, that sort of thing."

"What was the name again?"

Jacob looked in his Day-Timer to get it as the Detective had given it to him.

Ez tapped the name into his Smart Phone. And then made another entry and another. Mary, looking over his shoulder, was writing down names as he went,

"Wait. Ok, got it. No. Go with that one," she said.

After a few minutes, Ez announced. "Well I hate to tell you but Talent Enterprises is a subsidiary ... and he started down a list of companies owned by other ones who were owned by another all ending with the 5G grandparent in sunny Cayman Island."

"I think the thought plickens," Mary added with a grin.

"Look I made that mistake once. So, what if he works for a company that is owned by whoever. It doesn't make him a criminal, nor does it make Ms. Quinn any more guilty. She has a ticket that the office doesn't seem to know about. She just happened to do interviews on people who suddenly were kidnapped. She could have been followed. Suppose she does go to the casino; how could you link that to missing money at work? The only thing would be to catch her with a bundle of bank drafts from Lindsay Inc. *If* she had them. It is more likely they are with some hacker on the other side of the world.

Mary handed over a photograph, "Does that look like Ms. Quinn's briefcase?"

"Yes."

"No, you keep it." She waved the picture back to him. He waved it like the didn't know what to do then stuffed it into his back pocket. "She bought it in the first week of joining up with Ms. Maggie."

"When she took on her new duties as Research Head. Why wouldn't she need a new attaché case it makes sense to keep all her related materials, questionnaires, whatever, in such a secure and proper case. Would you expect her to carry such stuff in her purse? Or a grocery bag?"

Jacob stewed for all weekend and half the next week.

*

"Have you still got the picture?" TD asked when Jacob lamented his indecision the following Wednesday. Jacob hauled out the scrap that was still in his back pocket but under a handkerchief now.

Handsome," TD agreed. "You know if you think this lady is a criminal, she's about to break for it. We're down to a couple weeks till Christmas. You said she was finished her interviews which could be cover for her gambling and ..." he tapped a question into his phone, "Flights to Georgetown Cayman Islands are on Friday and Wednesday. If I were a thief doing this, I'd be headed out ... well today - certainly by next Friday. Hmmmm."

"So, she'll have an exit plan. Likely no luggage. Could also have an executive jet in her hip pocket and the scheduled airline ticket could just be a ruse. So how would you get to the airport if you weren't sure which you would need?"

"Are you asking me to think like a criminal?"

"No, a critical, thinking philosopher."

"Well I'd take a cab because I don't drive a car now."

"Right." TD began to chuckle. "Ok. Do you want to test if you are right or not?"

"About what?"

"Ms. Quinn of course. Do you want to test if she is going to leave this afternoon and whether she's a crook or not?"

Jacob didn't like the turn the conversation had taken from a confession to a conspiracy. He dithered.

"The worst that could happen is that you stand trial for a felony. The best is that you might save Ms. Maggie's bacon. And in between is the chance of becoming neither or both."

Jacob shook his head in confusion, "Look if she was a thief, she should be called to account. But I have no idea how to make that happen. I'm not going to get a gun or anything like that."

"How far would you go to help a friend?" TD asked. It was the question he'd asked Winston a while ago.

"I'd risk a lot for friendship," Jacob finally acknowledged.

"Even if it's rejected?"

"I'd know I did what was right."

"Ok," chuckled TD. "I want you to be in the lobby of Lindsay Tower by three o'clock - make it two thirty. Bring a book or magazine. If Ms. Quinn is leaving this afternoon, she'll be walking from the elevator that brings her up from the parking area before three thirty. She'll be walking fast and thoroughly ticked off. She'll exit the front door onto the plaza and head for a taxi at the curb"

"How can …?"

"Never mind. You just be there and be ready to give me a hand when I need you."

"To do what?"

"You'll figure it out. That way you can deny prior knowledge. See you later. Be on time."

Jacob felt little nauseous as he left, wishing the others of the Coffee Club a good day. What had he done?

25

Jacob declined the regular teaching staff invitation to the rooftop lounge/cafeteria. He was at Barak's elbow at two thirty in the lobby, as TD had asked.

"A friend asked me to meet him here but said he might be late and not to despair. If he was going to pick me up, he couldn't sit at the curb and wait. You know how the meter maids are. They've heard it all. NO sympathy. Bam! There's your ticket. 'You have a nice day now'."

Barak agreed. Eventually Jacob moved around to the side of Barak's desk facing the street. He was out of the way there and from that position he could also see the closed circuit monitors. He spotted Ms Quinn as she boarded the elevator upstairs, large designer bag on one shoulder, attaché case in the other peeking out from under a full-length suede coat draped over it. The suit looked white on the black-and-white monitor but it would be the grey jacket and slacks he'd seen her wearing with the elegant yellow blouse earlier. She got off in the parking area. Her car was first in the line.

The trunk lid popped as she approached. A flip sent the coat into a jumble on one side, the attaché case went carefully in the centre, shoulder bag on top. The car lurched a bit as she revved it up and backed out. The car stopped halfway through its turn. She got out and seemed to look at a tire on the other side of the car. The body language said it all.

She got back into her car and slammed it back into gear. A puff of smoke from the rear wheel led to the vehicle lurching forward to bang into the cement wall. No brake lights came on. The movement caught Barak's attention too.

"That hurt," he said referring to the probably dinted bumper.

She slammed the door angrily and gave it a kick that she regretted as she limped slightly to the back to retrieve her bags. Her hand went to her jacket pocket then her ear - phoning someone probably. With one bag in each hand she backed away. She forgot her coat.

At the elevator she stabbed at the call button several times and seemed about to head for the stairs when the elevator arrived with a load of others. She had to step aside to let them off.

"I'm sure she would have remembered that the door to the stairwell is locked if she tried it." Barak said. He'd been following the drama.

Motion on the street caught Jacob's attention. A taxi pulled into the marked stand and stood waiting. When she came off the lift, hair only slightly askew, Ms Quinn looked immediately to the street. Her steps seemed to speed up. If that cab was for someone else, she was going to commandeer it. She had to get there fast and first.

Jacob left his place and stepped across the lobby to the rotating door. Ms Quinn was halfway across the plaza making for the taxi with singular intention. The Meter Maid was already sauntering towards the taxi as though she had a countdown clock ticking off the time he could legally remain stopped there.

*

"She'll be out in a few minutes, Pete. Can we go over the plan for the last time?"

"Yeah," Pete said rocking a bit and focused on his shopping cart piled, as usual, with beer cans and his sleeping bag on top.

"You have to cut her off before she gets to the curb first, then dump your cart on top of her as though she knocked you over."

"Got it," Pete said softly.

"She'll drop her attaché case. It's like the one in the picture."

"Yeah," Pete said focused on his cart as if he was watching a movie.

"Get your sleeping bag over the case so it's out of sight and scoop both into the cart. Gotta be fast. Then you can start to pick up the cans. We'll get them all back before we go."

"It smells good," Pete said referring to TD's carryout tray with large coffees in all four sockets. Two hot dogs loaded with sauerkraut, mustard and ketchup were wedged between the cups.

"We'll go for more if the mission succeeds. It depends on you."

"I'll do it, sir"

"Good man."

They stood in the chilly corner a while longer till TD announced. "Target in sight. See her?"

"Yes sir."

"Go."

Pete stepped into action with uncommon speed. The shopping cart rattled as he hustled for the garbage can at the taxi stand. He was oblivious to anything else but the recycle stuff that might be in it.

That's what Jacob could see as he looked out from the lobby. Behind Pete was some guy in Friday-casual jeans and leather jacket his hat tipped against the breeze. He was carrying a bunch of coffees on a tray in one hand and a squared briefcase in the other. He was striding for that taxi too.

In the next moment it looked like a balloon of brown water burst over Ms. Quinn and the other guy dashing for the taxi. Pete was knocked off his feet, his load of recycle cans spaying in an arc following the water. The clatter trapped in the walls of the plaza sounded like a collapse in a can factory. Screams came from the jumble on the pavement. The guy in the leather coat staggered back knocked almost off his feet.

 "Good God woman," he shouted in English heavily accented. "Can't you watch where you're going?" He collided with the By-law officer who had run to the scene and caught him.

 "Did you see that, Officer? She bloody well knocked me off my feet and smashed this poor sod …"

Pete had set a terrible wailing as his precious load rolled around the pavement and blew into the roadway. He threw the sleeping bag into his cart once it was righted and howled in dismay as his treasures got kicked away by the accumulating crowd also trying to avoid the pileup.

 Jacob ran towards the jumble as the collision evolved. It was Ms. Quinn's screaming that had everyone looking up. "Get it off me," was repeated several times. Poor Pete was back on his feet, cart aright and scrambling to collect his stuff when Jacob arrived. Ms. Quinn was back on her feet but she was drenched with coffee, sauerkraut stuck in her hair, condiment stains streaked down her blouse and designer jacket. She was wide-eyed and hysterically wiping at the mess down her front. The By-law officer was trying to say something soothing, to no avail.

"Are you all right?" Jacob blurted out as he arrived and even as he said it, thought it had to be a rhetorical question. She was not.

"Does it look like it? This …" she couldn't find words, "smashed into me … and look at me …" She broke off into more enraged screaming, finger pointing and accusations.

Jacob had caught an arm to steady his incoherent colleague and realized something was catching his feet. He glanced down at the tangle he was standing on. He felt a crunch under his foot and inside the lady's shoulder bag but he stooped to pick it up anyway, quickly rising to say, "You dropped this." As he was doing so, he was already looking around. *Where was her attaché case?*

The case now scratched but secure lay a few steps away. At the same moment that he saw it and handed the shoulder bag to Ms. Quinn, she realized the case was missing.

"My case?" Quinn shrieked looking around. Jacob was already reaching for it. "My case," she screamed as though he was going to snatch it and run.

Jacob picked it up and held it out to her. She yanked it from his hand and shrank back. "You tried to steal my case," she shrieked.

In those seconds, the parking official had decided the man was not injured, only highly irritated that he'd lost his dinner and cab. "Sir," she shouted at the man fixing him with a threatening look and finger on her lips to cease the profanities.

The man threw down his hands in exasperation but stopped shouting mid-sentence. "Can I go," he growled. The officer decided that one less volatile temper on the scene was a good idea. "Go," she directed with a nod.

And then the drama over the attaché case distracted her.

She boldly stepped between Jacob and his accuser. "Ma'am I saw the whole incident. I think you were intent on getting to the taxi that was here and you collided with … this gentleman. I can see you are not injured but … you might want to change before going on." The comment drew attention to the soiled front. She was also shivering with the chill of being soaked or the aftereffects of the adrenaline rush, the officer observed. "Can we go into the lobby here while I call for help? You'll be out of the chill and …"

"I live here," the bedraggled woman spat. "I'll look after myself," and she turned abruptly and stormed off.

Pete had not stopped his piteous wailing as he collected cans around their feet. Jacob bent down to help him. The officer drew the lady aside continuing in as soothing a voice as she could. Pedestrian traffic was picking up as new arrivals entered the plaza and those who witnessed the event dispersed. Jacob ran out into traffic to gather a few flattened cans as Pete continued sweeping the space for missing items.

"There are three missing," mumbled Pete as Jacob surrendered the flattened ones. Pete put them in his cart and spotted one more crushed in the gutter.

The officer had turned from the retreating form of Ms. Quinn when Jacob saw them. "By the planter," he pointed to two silver eyes blinking in reflected headlights from the traffic. Pete darted off and Jacob turned to greet the official. She had to step out of Pete's way.

"I was waiting in the lobby," Jacob said. "I saw the whole thing," and he related it. He named the wet woman in his account.

"That's what I saw too. So, you know her? You called her by name."

"She works in there. Head of Research. I'm on the same staff."

"Bit of a temper, I think."

"She's really upset," Jacob replied. Pete was back with his lost cans. A biblical reference to lost sheep crossed Jacob's mind.

"If we can go, I'll take Pete along to the shelter. It must be dinner by now."

"I didn't know that was his name. But yeah, go along. I've seen him around forever. Never any trouble." Pete was already at the waste can at the curb checking it out for anything recyclable.

"Time to go, Pete," Jacob called. Pete returned with two liquor bottles to add to the cart.

"Let's do another turn around the place to check if we missed any." Behind the planter that the earlier finds had fetched up against, they found one more. They picked it up.

"It's a new one," Pete said. They rattled away Pete muttering to himself. Jacob thought he said, "Good job. well done," to himself and thought Pete was talking about getting all the cans back.

"Dinner at the Burger place," Pete said and turned that way.

"Sure, Why not."

Jacob was surprised to meet TD there.

"I brought you a bag for the cans," TD said when they met outside. "You put the cans in it and then come in. We'll get a table at the window. Leave your cart here so we can see it while we eat."

As they waited for their order, Jacob found out that Pete had once served with TD in the army. In fact, TD had been Pete's Commanding Officer when the incident happened that convinced TD to leave.

"I'll bring the order, you get the table," Jacob suggested. Pete was seated when Jacob returned with the coffee and desserts. The earlier bio information explained the greeting he overheard as he got to the table. "Well done soldier." He went off to the washroom. He saw TD taking off the gloves as he made his way back across the room. It seemed odd.

Dinner was hot dogs, lavishly decorated, apple pie and coffee. Conversation was a rehash of the moment in the plaza. TD stayed in his military persona. He called it a de-briefing.

"I didn't recognize you all dressed up as you were," Jacob said to TD. "And the accent. Where did that come from?"

"You learn many things as a soldier," was all TD would offer.

"So aside from delaying Ms. Quinn's departure, and I must confess it seemed to accomplish that, what exactly was achieved?"

The question seemed to catch TD off guard. "We have her attaché case is what we have."

"You stole it?" Jacob was aghast.

"She dropped it. You're going to return it."

Jacob could see the corner of the case now, sticking out from beneath TD's jacket on the bench beside him. "Maybe you'll get mine back. I think she picked it up by mistake. I've already reported it missing. It has my baseball card collection in it."

"But I gave it to her," Jacob blurted. "It was on the ground next to her - well maybe a few feet away."

"Well you're going to say you found it behind the planter where it must have been kicked in the confusion. There were a lot of people. It was only when I got home that I realized I didn't have my case anymore. That's why I called it in, to see if anyone had found it. Maybe your Research Department Head has mine."

"Are you sure that isn't yours?"

"My combination code won't open it."

Jacob wasn't sure his hot dog was going to stay down. His head buzzed with confusion.

"It is no big thing, Jacob. You just take it back to the concierge or if he's off, right up to your boss and say you found it after all confusion in the plaza. You weren't sure what to do with it. She'd been so rude, claimed you were trying to steal hers. Now you found a second one that looked something like hers, but you had already given hers to her. You just decided to bring it back and let someone else deal with it. Not your problem. Surely someone else is missing it. Be sure you have a witness when you return it."

He was not happy about it but that was what Jacob was going to do when he left the restaurant.

He tried to hand the case over to Barak so he could go home. It was not to be.

"Ms. Maggie called for the video surveillance of the plaza and I've just downloaded it, Barak said." He waved a USB. "I'll ride up with you. That was some commotion eh?"

"You wouldn't believe."

"Can I set this up on your monitor? Ms. Maggie?" Barak asked. He'd walked right in ahead of Jacob who was rooted to the floor just inside the office door. Across the room was Ms. Quinn flushed and grim-faced, elegant hairdo converted to plastered-down shower style. On the Maggie's desk lay an attaché case, scuffed and mustard-smeared in the seams of the leather.

"Could you stay and run the video for me?" Maggie asked of Barak. "We need to see what happened out there. Dallas says that her briefcase is missing and we have to see if the video picked up anything." She looked up and for the first time seemed to notice Jacob was standing there and in his hands was an identical attaché - well a similar one, no mustard stains.

"Be with you in a moment," she said icily to Jacob.

From his perch on the low table by the door, Jacob followed the video watched by the others on the far side of the desk.

"This is Ms. Quinn as she's leaving. Note the time stamp."

"And here comes the vagrant."

"Slow down."

"And there he is in front of you."

"Back up."

"Yep it looks like he cut you off and that you reached out …"

"Go back."

"You seem to be off balance. Did you grab for him?"

"I tried to twist out of his way."

"And then you turned into … Oh my, look at that."

The discussion continued as they traced the frame by frame movement of the case, out of sight but two frames later just where Jacob picked it up.

"But this isn't mine." Dallas insisted. "My combination won't open it. And mine had all the research data." Her voice was gaining strength and entitlement with each word.

"Back up to before the collision. Let's follow the other man."

"There he is. Can't see his face but you sure can see the coffee holder. Must be serving the office. Forward. Stop. Look he has a briefcase too. See it there just swinging out beyond his leg." Barak ran the series a couple times.

"So, can we follow it through the collision?"

"There was some painstaking silent study. "Nope. But yours lands right where you'd expect it after you dropped it."

"But if I had mine, it would open with my combination. This doesn't," Dallas spat, and spun the tiny dials on the latch to prove it.

"You're sure you got the right combination?"

"Do you take me for a fool?" Dallas hissed back, claws out.

"Maybe this is yours," Jacob said from the doorway. He tentatively held up the one he was holding. "I found it behind one of the planters after everyone left. I was helping Pete ..." He'd made his way across the room and set his case gently on the desk and pushed it carefully across to Maggie. "Maybe the video will show that if you go further. Pete is one of the street people I knew from the summer. He has a head injury and collects beer cans and liquor bottles. He is pretty fixed on his task."

They followed the rest of the video. "There he is picking up cans. That's Jacob helping ... and talking to the officer. Who is that officer?"

"Not Police - she is By-law - tickets anyone parked too long at the curb. She told us all to go home when there were no injuries. Ms. Quinn had already left by then. Jacob had backed up to the doorway again.

"Yes, I saw that," Maggie confirmed. "And here he is picking up the case from behind the planter as he said, can't see the case but what else would he be picking up?"

There was a silence till the clip ran out. "So, let's see if it is yours, Dallas. Put in the combination."

Dallas looked at the case as if it were a serpent. She stepped forward and slowly turned the wheels to align the digits. She fingered the catch and pressed.

Cl-clack went the double sound of bolts released. Clasps popped open.

"Whew," breathed Dallas and looked up brightly. "I guess I am in your debt, Mr. Eiger. The rosy glow beamed his way froze in midair when Maggie said.

"Open it. Just to be sure it hasn't been tampered with."

"Oh, I'm sure it is secure that's why it has a six-digit … "

"Open it." Maggie commanded.

"Don't you trust …"

"Open … it. Please." But it was not a request.

Dagger stares were exchanged. Dallas made the first shoulder shrug into a tantrum, picked up the handle of her case and spun to make her exit. But she had not snapped the clasps closed.

Bundles of money, envelopes with numbers on the cover, passports flew across the room. She bolted for the door.

Jacob was shocked at the whirl of paper and dodged sideways but stuck out a toe as Dallas passed. Crash! She went to the floor face down beside the receptionist's desk.

Jacob took one step and fell on both knees in the middle of her back crushing the wind from her, pinning her down. The Head of Research was helpless. The flailing arms and legs and screams said so.

26

"Let me out here," Jacob said. The patrol car pulled to the curb.

"You live here?" the officer asked pointing to the house.

Jacob was about to explain that his house guest would be in a panic if a police car pulled into the driveway.

"Yeah," Jacob said. He expressed his thanks and waited till the car was around the corner then walked the rest of the block to his house.

The light was still on in the living room. "I saved you some dinner but it is cold. I could zap it," Winston offered.

"I've never mixed a drink in my life," Jacob said from the doorway. "And I've resisted temptation left by my predecessor. But tonight, I am vanquished. Do you suppose you could mix up something from the cupboard? He pointed to the polished cabinet in the corner of the room." Though he had succumbed to the occasional drink at the pub a year ago, he had resisted the temptation behind the cupboard door. Until now.

"Let me try," offered Winston with a chuckle.

Jacob sagged into his favourite armchair and tipped his head back.

That's how Winston found him when he returned with a double scotch on the rocks - but sound asleep.

"Well can't let this go to waste," said Winston to the sleeping man in the chair. He put a blanket over the old man and took the drink to his own bedroom.

27

"It seems I misjudged you once before and repeated my mistake again." Maggie had invited Jacob to her office. Both were sitting on the sofa and because it was after work, Maggie offered a drink. To her surprise, Jacob accepted.

"Most people share that quality. Sad but true. I'm sorry for the heart hurt I caused you in the process. What everyone shared was their angst as they saw pieces of this sanctuary that you've built virtually single-handedly being threatened by someone playing on your best nature. I became the lightning rod, I guess. Would you care to know about the others who were instrumental in uncovering the deception?"

Maggie nodded and it became a monologue.

When he was done, both sipped at their drinks in silence. Maggie broke it, "I told you a while ago that I'd wanted to build a sanctuary for homeless or abused men, like this is for women. Do you think the men you befriended over the summer and who helped recover the funds that could make that dream a reality would be interested in consulting on such a plan?"

"I wonder if the problem would be getting them to stop laughing. You wouldn't believe the stories of exploitation I've heard. I think the big issue in deciding if they want to be consultants is the credibility of the task. I don't want to cast aspersions on your honest intentions. I'll be your ambassador but you have to realize where these guys have come from. They have suffered enough abuse to use up any faith they might have had in the system. Take one example I heard not long ago. One of the guys got out of prison. The deal is they return you in the community where you were arrested. So on exit day, you get to the gate with a bus ticket, whatever you might have earned working inside the prison, which is a scandal, and you get off the bus downtown. Your first job is to find a place to live. Without an address, you can't apply for a job. If you don't get a job, how do you live when the change in your pocket runs out."

He continued, "So, let's imagine that you are the most fortunate of men and find a rooming house in the first hour after you step into town and a job in the next. What do you do after work if you are exiled from your former friends? You can't go to the pub because that's where your buddies might be. You haven't got money for a drink anyway till after payday. It's hard to make new friends where you work when they find you've been in jail. You aren't called up to the Barbecue circuit. So, you walk the streets till you get tired. I did that. But the cops didn't stop me. They *did* stop the guy I'm talking about. Up against the car. Crime nearby, your MO, where were you last couple hours? Can you prove it? Come with us. If you fight the charge, he was told, the proceedings may take a year and more. Plead guilty and start serving time now. You could be out in nine months. See anything wrong there?" Jacob was getting red-faced. He drained the last of his glass.

"I think I caught a need for housing," Maggie said. "And maybe a job. Sounds like our system here."

"It's far from the total picture," Jacob said. "I don't know how many other groups are around. I don't know how effective they are. If they work so well, why are any of my guys on the street? There are dots not connected here."

"Well I'd be interested in talking to those who would like to contribute to making lives of men better - maybe theirs and the others they call friends.

"I'll pass the word." There was a pause. "Is that all.?"

Maggie looked away at the window. "You saved a dream - you and the others. We recovered most of the bank drafts, but the losses will sting forever. We found the flaws in the system that had been waiting to bite back. There are a lot of people who will survive because you and your bunch of merry men risked a lot to make it happen. Will you tell them all thank you?"

Jacob was standing by then. "Yes," he said. It was hard to say more.

28

"I don't think I ever saw that much money in one place before," Jacob admitted to TD. "Million-dollar drafts, money in bills I didn't know they made, fluttering around like confetti. In my whole life I've never earned the value of one of those bank things. Did you know that was in there?"

"Yeah. While you were in the bathroom. I tried a couple combinations. The one for the next day worked. That would be the day she was supposed to land in so much money even she could never spend it all. People are usually not very imaginative about passwords because they seem unable to remember them."

"What's your suggestion for making a password?"

"There are lots of military acronyms or epithets. Ordinary seniors should use nursery rhymes. Modern hackers never learned them. So, take something like Jack and Jill ..." It's easy to turn first letters of each word into a mix of letters, numbers and symbols. And no senior will forget it either. Tack on a short form for the place you use it, like 'bk' for 'bank', 'cc' for credit card, 'in' for 'internet' you get the idea ... and you're set. But you better write it down for others who might need to know it. Seniors sometimes have sudden changes and frequently they are serious."

Jacob had asked TD to walk with him along the river after coffee with the Club. "Did you really plan all that out? How did you know she'd have a flat tire?"

"I foretell the future … and assist it as needed." He pulled out his merchant marine fold-up knife. "Sidewall of a tire is no match. The timing was pretty predictable also. Who wants to get to the airport early especially if you have an ego issue? I knew she'd call a cab when her own car failed. The only part I worried about was you finding the beer can I left behind the planter. It was a 70-30 chance you'd pick it up."

"Pete said it was an extra, and I wondered about that at the time."

"Pete has a gift for numbers. He can tell you the number of cans in his cart any time you want and he'll be right."

"Maggie is motivated to start her sanctuary for lost men. She asked me to invite the coffee club to consult on the matter."

TD burst out laughing.

"I said you'd do that. But she's serious and this lady has steel. She'll do it the best she can so if you want to be part of the process instead of the critics, shut up and step up."

"You learn early, as a soldier, not to volunteer. When things go wrong, they fall from great heights upon the guy who stepped forward."

"So, I don't know why any of those guys complains about the bureaucrats that they moan about at every chance. The suits are doing exactly what they would do. Say nothing and follow orders. Not my fault. Here's a chance to choose the battlefield. Isn't that a good part of military strategy? Gather the forces, get them all marching in one direction, …"

"You been reading up on military history?"

"I just think there is such a wealth of experience in rough living that nobody outside the group knows or wants to know. The government social agencies seem to have canned solutions and are suspicious of everyone they minister to. Why is anyone surprised to find one solution doesn't fit all? What Maggie is offering is a chance to imagine and set guides that would work for the Club. Presumably, those plans would work for similar others elsewhere. To me, there is such variety in the group, that the range of solutions and the way they think about them, would work for a lot of others that suffer under their current situation."

"Maybe, but the problem is getting those who have been beaten up by the system, working together to change that same system. Given that miracles happen, what are the chances that the currently powerful solution providers won't dig in to resist loss of their jobs? As I see it the biggest issue is having any faith that the system we seek to improve won't turn around and bite back rather than change. It's really a credibility issue. The only weapon some of these guys have," he flicked a thumb over his shoulder toward the streets, "is continued resistance. 'You will not defeat me', sort of thing.

"Coraggio. Fede. Credenza."

TD started at the Italian terms. "Now I know you've been reading. Are you up to opera?"

"I've been infected, seriously."

"May you never recover. … But back to the other thing. Maybe after Christmas would be a good time. Let people think about it for a while."

"What does everyone do at Christmas?"

"Feel sad? Lonely? Cynical? Celebrate a free meal wherever it's available?"

"It sounds like La Bohème."

"We don't usually sing - the local company hasn't approached us - not that many could participate anyway, but some of us …"

"Might be a goal worth accomplishing."

"Jake, you are learning demonic habits. Been watching Faust?"

They were back at the start of the River Walk. Jacob had reached a decision. "Do you suppose The Club would join me for Christmas Dinner? Winston is already on the list. Would the others come?"

"It would be better than a bunch of alternatives."

"Give me a head count. They have to be single - no kids. Any allergies?"

"Allergies? That'll have them rolling on the ground." But he caught a breath and said with a straight face, "I'll ask," TD said with another laugh. "Talk tomorrow."

29

"Forty-five," TD said. "All said they could only eat gluten free."

Jacob's eyebrows shot up and his heart sank. He'd been expecting maybe a dozen at the outside.

"I'm just pulling your chain, Jacob. Everyone will eat whatever you serve and be glad. Can I suggest it be on Christmas Eve like midafternoon and end early? Many want to come but they do have other commitments," TD was being serious; Jacob was dismayed at the group size.

"Why not?" Jacob was still reeling. *How could he possibly host such a mob?*

"So, it will be at your house?"

"What kind of a castle do you think I live in?" Jacob's brain was buzzing. "Talk to me tomorrow."

In the next hour he contacted every hall and church in walking distance. Of course, all were not available for the evening - staff off to enjoy family time, or in use for the traditional pageant. One solution dropped on him like a waterfall of relief. *The Tower! Of course,* he thought and immediately the view from the penthouse lounge came to mind. Lots of space, food at hand, could schedule it between their meals. People who knew the kitchen and might cater it if he spoke nicely. And then. The showstopper - it's a women-only place. He'd never get this mob up there.

Well the head honcho might have at least a suggestion and he was fresh out of ideas.

Maggie responded quickly to his voicemail pleading.

"Well you certainly can't bring that many men to the Lounge. But we could host them in the Gym. We could clear access on the elevator to the school level at that time and we do have the staff to prepare and deliver the food. Our own celebration of Solstice will be done days before. Our staff won't serve or clean up, and maybe we could call it square for the effort some of them made to…"

"I'm sure that would be seen as fair, if there is anyone who keeps count."

"You serving alcohol?"

"It gets pricey if we do."

"The Company will go for non-alcoholic punch and one beer each if they want it. Water will be on the tables in pitchers."

"Some may not see beer as a gift, if you know what I mean."

"Yes."

"What's the menu and the Cafeteria manager will tell you what you can have."

He had it all arranged when he called TD back.

"They asked if anyone was vegan?" Jacob asked.

"I don't think I ever heard anyone ever ask that at any of the places I've been for a free meal. One menu fits all. Well they do respond to those with diabetic issues, if you ask, but I'm impressed. The guys will be talking about that forever.

"They will be photographed to get in. It is an internal security protocol. Never leaves the building. Just don't be surprised."

The alert had everyone dressing up - maybe worn, or out of fashion, but *nobody wanted to be in his grubbies*, they said.

Two in the group got to the elevator doors and froze. Winston was checking everyone on at the lobby end after they each got cleared and had to get TD's help. Each of the claustrophobes was convinced to do some deep breathing, go with TD only, and to hold their panic for a count to twenty. By then the doors would open and they'd be in the bright hallway with windows out on the world. It worked.

As each passed the bar and was offered a choice of beers - in a glass - they got a magic marker dot on the hand that reached for it. Only a few needed to have that explained. TD pinned the one who went back for a second - with his other hand.

"You screw this up and we don't get invited back," TD hissed in his ear as he handed the miscreant into the charge of another of his former comrades in arms.

There were no chairs at the circular tables; all the seating was pre-set in clusters of six or eight around low coffee tables or beside plants brought in to soften the appearance of the place. There was no Christmas tree. The men found spaces easily and Jacob noted that the groups changed as time went on.

Some tried out the climbing wall a few steps up before others called them back. Some looked for the balls to shoot hoops but when none were available. Everyone traded stories from another day. The place was a-babble with happy sounds.

Some men just sat. He could see the sad and bad memories fighting for attention. He went to talk or send someone every time he spotted them. The claustrophobics moved their chairs to a safe place in the outer hallway where they felt comfortable.

Winston had recruited help to serve the food. Jacob watched as he went over the serving size to give with each person.

    Jacob called for their attention and explained how he had not known he had so many philosopher friends. It brought a laugh. "But you are all welcome to join in this most elemental of celebrations - food and friendship. We are here as guests of the management of this place. I work in their school. It is a place of refuge and shared kindness. At this time of year, they recognize that the sun stays a few moments longer in the sky than it did yesterday. The light has returned and for that we can all be thankful again. Please move your chairs to a place at the tables and line up for the food at the end of the room. Winston will direct you. Tell him of your special needs." That started a burst of chatter about what special needs they could create to confuse the servers.

As they ate, Jacob circulated to ask how they enjoyed the meal, if they had input to offer about a men's residence, how they would spend the next few weeks. When it was time to go, he asked that they return their dishes whence they came and stack the chairs. Winston had already parceled up a few takeaway meals for those in special need. Even so there was food for Winston to take home for them.

One of the guys asked Jacob if he could take his beer glass with him. He said he'd like it as a souvenir of the time when someone offered him a beer in a glass. He couldn't recall it happening before and it made him feel like royalty. He wanted to remember that feeling. Jacob signed an IOU note personally and stuck it in the empty slot in the dishwashing tray.

Jacob asked Pete to wait outside if he wanted the empty cans, knowing full well he would. Winston had cleared up any leftovers and tied up garbage bags. The brooms came out and volunteers polished the floor

"See you at home," Winston said pulling his loaded fold-up shopping cart with him. He gave Jacob the bag with all the washed, empty cans flattened to fit and the number in black marker on the outside of the bag when he left.

Jacob checked the floor, flicked off the lights, and followed him down.

"All out?" Jacob asked of Barik as he crossed the lobby.

"Clear."

Pete was waiting. Barak had told him to bring his cart inside and behind his desk. He'd keep it safe.

30

He hadn't counted on going in, just walk on by. No crowds were there to steer him in. An idle thought came to him, *I wonder if Maggie is inside?*

That's how he found himself as he approached the church he'd been at a year ago, but now he was approaching it from the other direction. *How metaphoric,* he chuckled. *No snow this year; nothing to hop over, either.* Another secret laugh.

Molly Faithful had just been AMEN'd as he entered. The usher nodded to standing room in the corner.

New costumes, Jacob observed to himself. More elegant Wise Men and more ragged Shepherds was the local attempt to add authority to a story that maybe the powerful few felt was threatened. His eyes scanned the black backs for any sign of Maggie, starting under the candles now dripping into foil plates meant for meat pies. Nowhere.

When the service reached its predictable end and all were invited to attend the reception in the Hall, he wandered along. Cider was served from the same cut-glass bowl. The table of nibbles was distinctly commercial. *Those with the cooking skills seem to have retired, maybe died,* he thought. *Maybe they got ousted in a power struggle? Maybe they were not as enamoured as they once were with the task of making thousand-piece offerings to the kitchen.*

Nobody spoke to him as he stood with his cup where he had last year. Maggie was missing still. How come? *I'll bet the budget resolution committee is having an attack,* he thought. *Are those faces with frowns and wrinkled brows the ones that were happily gathered around her last year?*

He looked around one last time and set down his styrofoam cup. *Definitely a change in the kitchen contingent. No wash-up of mugs this year*, he concluded as he made his way to the door.

He was almost home when he noticed the bundled figure walking ahead. Long white coat, big fuzzy hood, hands were deeply thrust into pockets. By the time he caught up, he was sure he knew who it was.

He cleared his throat and coughed unnecessarily to alert the person that someone was coming from behind. He could have passed but checked his stride as he came abreast of the lady. "Hi. My name is Jacob," he said. It was a grim face that looked around the fur.

"I wondered if I'd bump into you," Maggie said with no joy.

"You look pretty down," Jacob replied slipping reflexively into counselling mode. *Reflect the emotion,* he thought.

"I was supposed to be on a sunny island enjoying a holiday I'd looked forward to forever." Maggie said without turning. "It just shows what happens when you take your eye off the ball."

"I hope you're not sorry for being human. If you are, you missed the turn back there. They were looking for you."

"I'll bet."

"And if you were counting on joining me for coffee as you did last year, I'm not going to walk all the way back there so we can do that. But I can offer you a glass of brandy and some really good fruit cake to go with it and the biggest ear you ever saw. Maybe cold comfort considering what you thought you might be doing, but it does match the surroundings. My roommate has recently taken care to culture my enchantment with fruit formerly forbidden. There was a time when I was sneaking it like a thief, but with Winston's help, I'm learning to enjoy a drink. Tonight's libation is in celebration of the Passing of the Solstice, you know. Every day gets brighter and longer from now."

"Who's your roommate?"

"Winston is his name. He was the guy who rang the bell on the kidnapped women and where they were. I offered him a place to stay instead of the warehouse. He also took the leftovers back to our house if you fancy a late dinner. There's lots.

"I was watching you on the closed-circuit feed. You were doing all the glad-handing as people left. I saw him doing the clean-up, scalloped potatoes into one container, turkey into another. He really seemed organized. Is he a cook?

"Probably not. He learned kitchen skills along his way."

"Ok, I'll take you up on the offer."

"Walk on," Jacob said. "Walk on with hope …"

"I know how that song ends," Maggie said, "and it ends wrong … ly."

31

"This really goes nicely with the Brandy," Maggie complimented as she took another slice.

"Fruit cake has gotten a bum rap ever since the commercial product hit the shelves. They skimped so badly they made it into a mockery but it's all anyone knows - except for we who make it. The light cake goes well with the drink too."

"Well don't mind if I do but my glass will need a top up."

Jacob reached across with the bottle and splashed a generous refill into the bulbous glass.

"What kind is that?" She leaned to turn the bottle to see the label.

"No idea. The former owner left it along with a well-stocked cabinet of other liquors. Is it a surprise he was a cleric?"

"Probably Anglican or a closet drinker."

"Well he wasn't Anglican, I know that - least he wasn't when he left to study overseas." Jacob took another sip. "The liberal ways into which I've wandered philosophically have been accompanied by an admiration of fruits long frowned upon. Anyway, here's to the return of the sun. Brighter days ahead." He lifted his glass.

"I'll sure drink to that," Maggie said, and downed the remnants in her glass in a big gulp. She was reaching for the bottle and stopped midway, paused and fell back into her seat. "That's enough," she said almost to herself.

"I'm sorry that she turned out to be such a …

"Me too. I'm more sorry that I made such a complete fool of myself. All the behaviours I'd learned for years that kept the Foundation safe and secure … Well it won't happen again. Even if I do a nosedive, the procedures are in place to set off bells at the first sign of irregularity." She raised a hand to reach for the bottle and again yanked it back.

Jacob handed over the remains of the cake plate and picked up the bottle when she took the cake. He moved it back to the cupboard out of sight.

"I've been talking to some of the men about your consulting offer," Jacob began. "Some are skeptical; some are just out to screw up anything that sounds like the system that they feel beset by. But I think we've shaved off those edges."

"Those that have a place that they can rent with what income they have are always looking for something better. Not many have apartments. They really need a place to keep their stuff, a place to get out of the weather. You'd probably call it junk, but it is theirs and it was usually hard gotten." Maggie was looking into her empty snifter and raised it to smell the residual aromas within the glass.

Jacob continued, "Well they seek a space they can afford first. Money is everything. What they get is minimal - often cracked plaster and peeling paint, barely big enough to swing a cat. What they'd like has a bedroom with a private bathroom and shower or tub, a place to sit with a friend, maybe a place to make a meal. Except for Winston, I haven't met anyone with much kitchen skill. Most are big on processed food, TV dinners. Actually, I suspect they seek out the community dinners not only because of the cost but because of the social contacts they can make. And that brings up another side of the social thing. In listening to the many tales from the summer, the thing that seemed too common is there is not much to talk about that I'd call edifying. They might have dodged a misdemeanor, beat a competitor at cards, but not much I would call soul lifting. Little new has entered their lives that they could point to with pride if you take away the negatives. I guess their lives seem so parallel to the one I had till this year. I wish I could share that feeling of liberation, elation."

Jacob realized he'd been leaning forward to make his point. He sat back and shook his head, "Sorry, I was getting wound up. All this doesn't address how blue you are."

"Hearing your excitement is a relief," Maggie admitted. "But it does tell me how far I've fallen."

"Then maybe what I offer is how a friend like you lifted one like me, out of exactly where you are. You have many around you stretching out their hands.'

They sat is silence for a few moments before Maggie brought it to an end.

"Before I hear your suggestion that the inn has no room and that the stable is available, I'm going home," Maggie said as she stood abruptly and swayed a bit.

Jacob jumped up. "Let me call … Never mind. I'll see you home. You won't get a cab tonight. I'm not tired enough yet anyway."

32

It had been a quiet walk home. Maggie was so lonely despite his company. She missed the happiness she'd had and the person she had been then. What stretched out ahead of her was pushing a heavy rock up a long and steep hill - at least that is what he thought she saw.

He had felt the same only a year ago, in fact, and had been walking these same streets with the same load. He'd been disowned by all he had known because he'd dared to share discoveries that had excited him. His confrontation left him in loneliness that could have swallowed him but she had thrown him that lifeline when she introduced herself. As he walked home, he saw himself more as a plank or piece of the boat that had just sank under her.

It didn't bother him that he had all the direction of flotsam. As he mused on the thought through more steps, he considered that over the year he'd become a bigger plank. *Poor analogy. Wreckage doesn't get bigger.* But he felt like a solid plank, something that had been carefully crafted to fit into the bigger thing. It was just that now, when he had floated free of all that, he was the subject of curiosity. He didn't fit his new environment.

So rather than grow into a bigger board, he'd just picked up new decorations from the water he was drifting on. Barnacles here, seaweed there, a fishy companion or two to graze on the fuzzy stuff growing where a polished sheen had been. "That sounds better," he said to the empty street and he laughed at the way he was building a sermon for a phantom congregation.

He began to see the swirl of people and places in which he now lived as ... *what was that place in the Pacific where currents brought tons of discarded plastic ... a gyre? Yes, that was it.*

He was in some sort of social gyre pushed by randomness. He could feel the old tug to tuck God into the equation and laughed at himself. Old habits do die hard.

So, the question was how all this stuff, brought together by chance, might bring comfort if not meaning to itself. Maggie still thought of herself as the motor that was going to move the mess along. He had to admire her for that even if she was feeling dead in the water at the moment. But she was working in the boiler room, he could tell from her frowning silence as they walked.

When he suggested that the new men's residence actually be a collection of shipping containers, fitted out by their inhabitants to meet both code and personal needs, she hadn't scoffed at it. "They could be built on the ground, by the men themselves perhaps, with proper help. I wouldn't want one to cut off a finger. It might waken an interest that would be self-sustaining. Certainly it could put some of their own skin in the game - demonstrate a commitment." *I wonder if they all would work on their own place, even help each other? Was that better than wandering the streets?*

"When ready, the home units could be hoisted on a round-table elevator that could arrange habitations on the different levels like petals on a flower. Each residence could hook up to services in the building core like the botanical namesakes. Put the traditional businesses on the lower floors for the income that would pay the mortgage. Have a penthouse cafeteria and lounge that looked out over the neighbourhood instead of at the dumpsters that some said were outside the windows were they now lived. If it doesn't work out, and they all moved off to suburbia, the containers could be removed and the building's skeleton repurposed." He could tell she'd liked the anatomical reference by the snort that punctuated her silence.

The thought of using cast-off shipping containers reminded him, yet again, of the Diogenes Barrel story - about him living in one to scorn the consumptive excesses he saw around him but he liked the flower image better. It led to the tingle he so enjoyed as he remembered feeling like he had awakened and opened to the new life that had emerged from the wreckage. Yes, he embraced uncertainty now, felt its promise and potential compared to the security-ruled rigidity and certainty, however incredulous.

He compared what he called faith now with what he'd had back then. Now he had to believe in the goodness of those about him rather than promises built to justify statements made by people in a power struggle. Which took more faith - to believe you didn't know nor could not, or that slavish following of a rule book would produce a heavenly payoff? He'd solved that one to the satisfaction of the intellect he had that came with his eyes and nose. He could live with it.

And with profound enlightenment achieved, he spotted the porch light that beckoned him.

Jacob found Winston watching a seasonal favourite on Television when he got home. "Guest for dinner tomorrow," Jacob announced.

"Time?"

"I suggested come for a drink about four thirty, eat about six."

"That's supper, not dinner," said Winston without looking away from the screen. "So, guest for supper, right?"

Jacob grimaced. *Remember. Peace on Earth* he thought. "Yeah."

"Did you tell the guest it was leftovers?"

"She knows."

"Say Winston," what do you think of the idea of building your own apartment?

Winston turned with raised eyebrows, his television program forgotten. "Pardon?"

Additional Titles by K.G. Watson
Shop www.pandamoniumpublishing.com/shop
Duty's Son
Duty's Daughter
Duty's Dad
Acts of Remembrance
Life Supports

CPSIA information can be obtained
at www.ICGtesting.com
Printed in the USA
LVHW051951070622
720715LV00020B/369

9 781989 506264